THE CELESTIAL BANDIT

A Tribute to Isidore Ducasse,
the Comte de Lautréamont,
Upon the 175th Anniversary
of His Birth

Edited by
Jordan A. Rothacker

KERNPUNKT • PRESS

ISBN-13 978-1-7343065-5-2

KERNPUNKT Press
Hamilton, New York 13346

www.kernpunktpress.com

Dedicated, as always, to Jessica

And

With deep gratitude to Jesi Buell for making this book happen

And

To Faisal Khan for being the driving spirit behind this project

Contents

Jordan A. Rothacker

Introduction

Dear Reader, it took me a long time to get into the Comte de Lautréamont and his delightfully weird and evil little book, *The Songs of Maldoror/Les Chants de Maldoror*. This might seem strange since I am editing a collection of tributes to this mysterious writer, but somethings you can't force. What is clear here is that once I do get into something I dive deep. I fall hard when I love someone or something. And here we are.

*

I first heard of Comte de Lautréamont through an interview with William T. Vollmann. I was a huge fan of Vollmann in college (still am) and sought to understand him and his work through his influences. Lautréamont was an important influence, not only on Vollmann's penchant for long, bursting-at-the-seams sentences, but also on shifting narrative voices, meta-textuality, and a love of gothic, Romantic darkness, to name a few. I gobbled up so many new writers and books from influences and favorites that Vollmann mentioned in interviews, educating myself further than any college curriculum could, and yet I couldn't get into Lautréamont's main work, *Maldoror*. Frankly, it frightened me, and I didn't get it. I couldn't see what the big deal was around all the evil and violence, which as I said, kinda frightened me.

*

It was Roberto Calasso who finally sunk the hooks into me. His words found the pressure point. (I mix my metaphors, but I am no Lautréamont). I was also a good bit older when I read *Literature and the Gods* (Knopf, 2001) in which we find a chapter on Lautréamont called, "Musings of a Serial Killer." In this essay he describes *Maldoror* as "the first book and that's no exaggeration—written on the principle that *anything* and *everything* must be the object of sarcasm." He goes on to exalt this book as going farther than any Romantic Satanic lit-

1

erature before it in depictions of violence and evil, and how it more importantly deals in repetition, plagiarism, self-plagiarism, and self-negation. Beyond *Maldoror* itself, in regard to parody, Calasso tells us Lautréamont "left not a single sentence—not even in his letters—that we might with any confidence *take seriously*." This sense of play and sovereignty over a text and all texts before it is not only proto-post-modern, but for Calasso emblematic of a shadowy concept he investigates as "absolute literature." In Lautreamont's second and final work (published under his given name), the *Poésies*, this work is continued through plagiarizing and "correcting" famous passages of works by authors of the Western canon who came before. Calasso describes Lautréamont as someone "inspired by the blasphemous craving to see what would happen if [he] poured scorn on absolutely all the rules... After [him] every philosophy and every literature would be shot through by a fatal flaw." Yes, Dear Reader, this was my point of eager entry, and I was finally ready.

*

It was then that I made the point to get the gorgeous, and extremely thorough, complete works of Lautréamont translated by Alexis Lykiard published by Exact Change in 1994. This single volume contains *Maldoror, Poesies*, and all of the letters history has left us by and pertaining to Lautréamont. There is also an introduction by Lykiard about Lautréamont and his work, notes on the primary texts, and a bibliography invaluable for scholarship. One category in the bibliography that covered "Critical (Books Dealing in Part With Lautréamont) mentioned Aimé Césaire's *Discourses on Colonialism*. It was a work I had read before, but somehow missed the Lautréamont reference. This moment here, thanks to Lykiard, was a defining point in the research for my doctoral dissertation in Comparative Literature in which I bridged Post-Colonialism and Romanticism. The dark-skinned revolutionary responding to colonialism was fighting the same battle as the Romantic poet in opposition to bourgeois capitalism. They both were subjected to flawed Enlightenment ideals.

*

Soon the references confirming my new love and devotion were everywhere. Albert Camus deals with Lautréamont in

The Rebel. Georges Bataille intentionally doesn't in his *Literature and Evil.* I remember, or notice anew, references to Lautréamont in works of some of my favorite musicians like John Zorn and Mike Patton. Walter Benjamin exalts Lautréamont in his 1927 essay on "Surrealism;" and of course, the Surrealists loved Lautréamont. That love and influence continues in a straight line to the Situationists. Specifically, Guy Debord employed the technique of detournement from the *Poésies* for his book *Society of the Spectacle.* And once when digging deep into a biography on Amedeo Modigliani, one of my favorite painters, I read that he often carried a copy of *Maldoror* in his pocket and would drunkenly shout passages at passing carriages in the streets.

Eventually I learned that Maldoror was on David Bowie's top 100 list of favorite books. Bowie was a brilliant, precocious weirdo, just like Ducasse. The first Chant, or chapter, of *Maldoror* was published in 1868 when Ducasse was twenty-two, the same age as Bowie when he recorded "Space Oddity." I want to punch those kids, those brilliant brats. Not physically, but metaphysically as Artaud would say.

*

For the uninitiated it is a brief life and career to summarize. Isidore Ducasse was born in 1846 in Montevideo, Uruguay where his father, Francois Ducasse, was a consul for the French government. His mother died when he was an infant, and he was raised by his father in Montevideo until the age of thirteen when he was sent to school in France. We know of his school records and from letters, his voracious reading habits that involved the canon along with heaps of Romanticism and gothic literature. After schooling, there was a brief return to Montevideo before settling in Paris in 1867 with an allowance from his father and the goal of being a writer. He self-published at first just the first Chant of *Maldoror* in 1868 and then the whole work of six Chants the following year. He took his pseudonym, with a slight alteration, from Eugene Sue's 1838 gothic novel *Latréamont* whose eponymous character bears some resemblance to Maldoror.

Ducasse followed his first book, a book about a serial killer who relished in evil and iconoclasm—a work of dizzying sentences, meandering digressions, shifting perspective, surreal language, and wide-ranging literary references—with a book devoted to goodness. The *Poésies* was self-published in 1870, and in it we find selections from classics of the Western canon like Dante Alighieri and Immanuel Kant, French writers like Pascal, La Rochefoucauld, and Hugo represented, and even a passage from *Les Chants de Maldoror*, all inverted and changed for the better to promote goodness. Ducasse died on the 24th of November later that year alone in his hotel during the Prussian siege of Paris. He was twenty-four years old and this year, 2021 marks the 175th anniversary of his birth.

*

Maybe, Dear Reader, you have come to this with no knowledge of Lautréamont or his work, but with an interest in one or more of the contributors? Whether you are familiar with this subject of tribute or not, this anthology is just full of some really great writing. You will find poems in direct tribute; poems inspired by Maldoror's uniquely evil voice; short stories about the young man behind the work; short stories and prose poems continuing a narrative within the world of *Maldoror*; essays on the importance of Ducasse/Lautréamont; an essay on how this literature can influence a genre as different as music; an essay on the difficulty of translating *Maldoror*; illustrations based off the only remaining photograph of Ducasse; and even an entry of neologisms inspired by Ducasse's use of subversion and detournement in the *Poésies*. Some of the contents are almost unclassifiable, a point I think Ducasse would enjoy. I feel honored to be in the company of these great artists, and to share in this crazy love.

*

My wish for you, Dear Reader, is to take this book in as a whole, maybe in a linear, alphabetical order and let the facts about Ducasse/Lautréamont and the art he has inspired wash over you in turn, an ebb and flow of limited certainty and introspective abstraction, a swelling sea of what pure creation can bring forth. The title is from the fifth chapter, or Chant, of *Maldoror*. Here we find our narrator confronting his place in the universe and the nature of his creator. It is a Job-like moment. The narrator refers to the creator as a Celestial Bandit and follows by saying, "If I exist, I am not another. I do not admit this equivocal plurality in me. I want to live alone in my intimate reasoning. Autonomy… or let me be turned into a hippopotamus. Sink underground, O anonymous stigmata, and reappear to my haggard indignation no more. My subjectivity and the Creator—it is too much for one brain."

As I propose, Celestial Bandit is also a term that perfectly fits Ducasse and how he presides over his literary realm.

*

Also, Dear Reader, it should be noted that there is a scene in the second Chant in which the character Maldoror rescues a female shark outnumbered in a battle with other sharks. Maldoror and the female shark swim together and he recognizes in her a wickedness greater than his own. In a beautifully rendered and hilarious passage, they bond, embrace, and eventually make love. It is clear from many entries within this anthology that you now hold that this scene has left a significant mark on certain readers.

Mark Amerika

Other Lives by DJ Lautréamont

Today I am a novelist inventing imaginary solutions for problems that don't exist.

Yesterday I was the lead vocalist for an impromptu jazz ensemble called *Electronique Écriture* (we have since broken up).

The day before that I was a sentimental art historian shamelessly disfiguring the pronouns of every gender that tried to identify itself with whatever slender thread of intuition that dared to occupy my fleeting operational presence.

The day before that I was a creative truant, a poster-boy for pure gluttony, eating two breakfasts (a bowl of quinoa-corn flakes with grapes, raspberries, strawberries, mango, banana, plums, blueberries, blackberries, figs, raisins, dates, and soy milk [all organic/bio, naturally] and a huge poppyseed bagel with smoked salmon and cream cheese), two lunches (new age ginger and vegetable pasta followed by North African vegetarian couscous with numerous [spicy] side dishes), one midday snack (*salade nicoise*), a small loaf of organic multi-grain walnut bread, a round of fresh Chevré with chives, two mangos, one and a half avocados, a slab of sesame-almond tofu, two bottles of Comte de Montebello Bourgogne Pinot Noir, a rare Belgium beer nicknamed Fencing the Moon made by organic monks (yes, the Trappist monks themselves are also organic!), five cups of Fair Trade Midnight Blend espresso (my stomach insisted this was all totally *unfair* but, alas, I rule over it, not it over me), two thick bars of 76% Venezuelan extra bitter dark chocolate, actually make that *two* loaves of organic multigrain walnut bread (with hummus and cilantro pesto liberally spread atop their lightly toasted crusty textures), one cup of real hot chocolate (not the usual "pre-mix watered down with milk" variety, but basically melted dark chocolate with a small amount of lightly ejaculated goat's milk mixed in so that it pours into the back of my throat like a silk disease), a double scoop of artisan ice cream (bottom scoop praline made with pine nuts, top scoop made with figs which turns the ice cream a luminous bright red so that you feel as though you are sucking the velvet blood out of a passive [dare I say virginal?] victim), one half of a strange yellow-orange melon whose name escapes me right now, a Zen-Zombie smoothie (peach, mango, banana, soy milk, quaaludes), three servings of ratatouille served over brown rice with a side dish of rocket (arugula) topped with fresh cherry tomatoes and thinly sliced Parmigiana cheese preserved in the bowels of an Italian mummy that I always come home to, a bowl of cured black olives soaking in extra-virgin (dare I say cold-pressed?) olive oil with a hint of rosemary and thyme, five pistachio baklavas, and a homemade Uruguayan chayá that serves as my madeleine involuntarily reminding me of my youth in Montevideo where, as the son of a French consular, I lost myself in an imaginary hyperobject of pathological desire ripping the cosmos to shreds. I ate many other things that I can't remember (wait! how could I forget? the faux potato latkes made out of *okara* at this very strange hole-in-the-wall Japanese take out joint with ginger-soy dipping sauce that I would now give half my non-existent salary for), especially after the unexpected hit of Absinthe that one of my sophomoric colleagues insisted I drink as a way to get over pining about how the melancholy struggle between good and evil, or faking a stream of tears that do not come from the heart but are programmed to manipulate emotions as if generated from an algorithimic machine, creates, everywhere, a universal void.

Tomorrow I will be a producer of the ultimate pleasure one derives from becoming the kind of Über-sexy, "live currency" one spontaneously transmits through an always-emergent networked space of flows if they ever hope to destroy the replicant agenda of the all-consuming corporate automata that perpetually consumes whatever primitive form of creativity I happen to latch myself onto while chanting my verse.

For now, though, I must take leave of my senses and allow them to be overrun by the smothering swarm of labia lips she has promised to entomb me with.

(DJ Lautréamont is a proponent of critical media literacy, professorial hacktivism, and practice-based research in the innovative arts. A former Chair in a Department of Fine Arts, he has since taken early retirement and now plays his DJ sets at low-key parties and occasional alternative gallery openings.)

Louis Armand

DISSECTION D'UNE FEMME ARMÉE
the dark feverdream returns from the past to torment

La saison violente / Notice: Use of undefined constant cum-shark -- assumed 'cumshark' in Lautréamont spa parlour / the first thing was blank non=pigment intruding on dark eurasian morass / neither male nor female neither MAL D'HORREUR nor MALODOROUS / such sweet mellifluent cunts smiling back at you from the waves / ma petite vierge=loup bien baisée / as blassé as a virgin thrown to the sharks / scaling knife slipping up under the sea wolf's gills... sliced out in bas relief / their eyes had been cordoned off (literature was a crime scene it was the only way it cld continue existing) / the plot drove flagrantly at high speed into the cul-de-sac, spreading the cheeks for a "Virginia Woolf" / is that the worst you can do? there was an amputated penis rotting inside, at first mistaken for a mummified rat / ritual had already taken the place of myth long before the procedure entered the textbooks / like a Freudian "bad penny" turning up in the queerest places (just how bad cld Penny get?) / more ante was demanded if Kapitalism wasn't simply going to shit itself to death: "demand feeds demand" / embodiment was just something they talked about in theory / le dernier Eden, par example / solo improvisations on the theme of shark attack erotica / a mouth full of asbestos: "I take on the limits of oceanography itself" / their world was like the wreck of the Titanic run aground (believing all humxn beings carry within them the potential to die harmoniously to an upswell of violins) / Übermarionette meanwhile drives the humxn actor from the stage, its "I of memory" / consider the timeless reverberations of gravitas in space: drifting, devolving, disintegrating, an eye for the vortex of an eye /first zero then nothing / their mother's love

9

Ben Azarte
The Shark Child

On the beach, at just the edge of where the sea marches before its retreat, are two children. One boy lay with his arms splayed as if tanning his torso. The whites of his eyes stare up like eggs divested of their yolks. From the gaping hole in his stomach, his blood soaks the sand around him. The trail of innards from within the boy lead to the mouth of the other sitting upright next to him. In his mouth full of numerous, razor-sharp teeth, he happily chews on the large intestine of his mutilated companion. His skin, soaked in the other boy's blood, is a mix of flesh and scales. His hands are webbed, keeping the blood and chunks of meat from sliding between its fingers. As he devours his meal, he reflects upon how he was able to trap this prey.

When he had swam from the deep blue loneliness of the sea and towards the shore, he happened upon a barefoot boy around his own age playing on the beach. He approached the boy, keeping his teeth hidden, and introduced himself. The boy was happy to meet him, unconcerned about his unusual skin. The two played in the sand, joyful and innocent as any other children. The boy from the shore showed the boy from the sea how to craft castles from the wet sand. When the boy from the shore confided that he could not swim, the boy from the sea taught him. They ran in the warm sun to dry themselves off. They rested and watched the sun begin its descent into the horizon where the sea meets the sky.

The boy from the sea confided in the boy from the shore of his past. He was the product of an unholy union of a human male and his shark mother. He was rejected by the other sharks in the ocean for his strange appearance. When he sought companionship on the shore, he was rejected by humans for frightening them. He had been for years and years without a single friend. The boy from the shore also confessed that he was a lonely child. He often found himself ignored by other children and his parents paid him little attention. How fortunate that these two lonely souls from such different places should meet. The boy from shore's face shone with the brightest smile the boy from sea had ever seen. He returned smile, showing the rows of teeth like blades in his mouth.

Then he lunged.

As the sun had disappeared halfway behind the edge of the sea, the boy licked the blood of his former best friend off his webbed hands. He reached back into the gaping wound of torso and ripped his liver out. He sank his pointed teeth into it, his body shaking with ecstasy at the flavor.

For a creature that spawned from the evils of a human and the endless bloodlust of a shark, no spice was more delicious for a meal than betrayal.

duncan b. barlow

A Different Kind of Vulture

1.
Along the abstract edges of a singular dull cloud, a kettle of turkey vultures hovered cowardly over the scent of something too slow or dimwitted to cross the road without penalty. The carcass, bloating and rancid, once had blinking eyes, had been a thing children wanted to touch, adopt, a dog or cat or armadillo, had once experienced joy in the way animals do. Perhaps these birds are enviable creatures, instinct driven things untethered to conscience and morality, free to act without fearing the long train of punishments constructed by man. People are pitiable creatures, acting and reacting out of fear of violating arbitrary social contracts. I may seem a fearful thing as I handle language with caution—forever revising my words in silence—but I assure you that I am not.

2.
I let my lover speak first, let him use language carelessly in a moment of distraction, so I may counter him, so I may tell him he is wrong, so I may send him backpedaling into submission. A careful dance—a nudge too far and his defenses strike with barbed lashes—I dexterously dissect his words, his tone, his body language. Just the other night he asked me to stroll with him along the river bank during those crepuscular hours where alligators along distant banks feast. It had been too hot during the day, and though we lived in a small flat along the edge of city center where there are shaded parks and the locals swim in the shallows of the river, we hid inside without speaking a word to one another, both occupying those parts of the apartment that we'd unofficially deemed our own—meticulously organized, cleaned, and arranged, mine a nest of comforts stacked and stuffed for convivence. It once concerned me that I often left things intentionally messy to provoke my lover into cleaning so I could rain insults down upon him. After all, I'd attended gymnasium where I'd been educated on empathy so I knew that my desire to provoke my lover was, objectively speaking, at odds with the consensus view of that which is deemed humane, but this concern

waned with each instance and soon turned to something else altogether, some pleasure that I am only now defining. We didn't speak for most of the walk, listening instead to the dismal sounds of our own footsteps and the shift change between cicadas and crickets. The air, though cooled with the coming of night, seemed immovable as we pushed through it. I, for lack of a better phrase, laid in wait for him, his stupid mouth, his need to speak to quiet those thoughts in his head telling him things he did not want to make manifest—that we have nothing to talk about, have nothing left in common, he is an aging relic with diminishing prospects and may never find another one like me or better. Then he spoke, commented on the swans swimming in formation on the river. I cannot explain to you why this is so, but I found a wave of pleasure wash over me when I let those words sit in the heavy summer air. (Though it's not quite pleasure that I feel as it doesn't make me feel good, but perhaps fills me with an uncanny goodness that cuts two ways and thus makes it all the more exhilarating).

3.
There was the incident with the boy. A child playing in the sandy bank of the river. He, busy scooping sand into a cup—building a small village—and my lover, sipping his tea, watched him with wonder. I knew he wanted a child, he wanted to share our home, as impossibly small as it is with a child so he might know a love that is unyielding, a love he did not receive from me. Admittedly, I had entertained the idea for some time. The two of us with a child, forever deflecting questions about the actual nature of our relationship or where the child had come from. But I had grown so old and my body tired, and though I did feel I could love, at least hoped I could love something, the idea of the child asking for things incessantly, launching into tantrums, forever needing attention drove me to distraction. Then, as if summoned by this very thought, the boy's mother pulled him from his place of wonder and the child screeched, a sound akin to the unforgiving cry of a rabbit torn asunder. As they passed me, the mother jerking the child's arm, the child resisting and screaming, I could not help but slip my foot out, just enough, to catch the edge of the boy's sandal, sending him stumbling to his knees upon the concrete. Forgive me, I pled, I didn't see your child. Let me buy him a sweet. Let me buy you a tea. I did this with my lover too after clubbing him about the head for days with insults, or after isolating him with silence.

I would perhaps make a meal for him, or take him to the opera, massage his back and feed him chocolates. Perhaps I tripped the boy because he was a nuisance or perhaps I did it because I knew it would pain my lover to see the boy suffer.

4.
Some days the wind howls fiercely and carries matts left for thrashing away from our modest balcony. Today is no such a day, the stifling heat undoubtedly aiding in the putrid vents' speed or odor intensity, calling more vultures to the cauldron to undulate in thermal updrafts. Should he return, I will ask my lover on a walk, lead him to the body of whatever it is that calls these hideous creatures, with their feathered shawls and naked heads. I am balding, my neck slung low from poor posture, I too am a pitiable thing, but I am no turkey vulture. I am a Black Vulture. My hands hungry to tear at things and pull them to my nest upon this sheer crevasse. My lover is wholly human and exhibits at nearly every turn striking examples of human kindness. When I tripped the child, for example, my lover injured himself trying spare the child from the pavement. As he limped home beside me, he told me of a dream where we both lived in home made of gold perched on the side of a mountain top.

"You ate me up."

"It was a dream."

"I felt myself in your bowels."

"I cannot continue to listen to you and your dreams."

"Rotting, I felt myself rotting."

I do not dream. There are no golden domiciles, no meals, no secret meanings. I close my eyes and I open them to a new day. I do not dream of better futures. I am a creature of instinct. Dreams are for unhappy men with foolish notions of potential futures.

5.
I work not at the behest of emotion. It does not serve me well. I've watched others needle endlessly at the fraying edges of their feelings and seen it sap them of their best interests. I am bound by my own logic and toil only away at that which

serves me best, and if others, such as my lover, offer freely their emotional weaknesses, I'm all too happy to avail the opportunity for gain. If I should live in a building made of gold and Cycads, it will be because of my cunning and not from my lover's emotions. Should he return, I'm of the mind to tell him as much and a good many other things I've thought since his leaving.

6.
When my lover left, he said very little. He looked out the window and mouthed something tight lined that blossomed into a black hole between his lips. His teeth were clean, his breath minty, everything about him delightful. I'm not without desire and I can assure you in that moment after my comment, after his reaction, I was filled with an ardent need that hindered my breath, and when I raised my hands to pull his head into them, to drive him to the ground in a tangle of passion, he stepped away and left. As the daylight drained from the room, I stood there, and when it again returned, I remained—steadfast in my belief he would return after having some time to think and I wanted to be there and conscious when he did. He'd done this before—admittedly only for a few moments, locking himself away in the bedroom only to emerge as if nothing had happened.

7.
My lover, who drank only pre-bottled water from the store, said he couldn't drink our tap water. He said, "I taste blood. I taste my own death." I am not without reason. For example, when I'd grown weary of glass bottles huddled in clusters upon our porch, I threatened to drop them off the edge, but he argued that we always needed the return deposit and despite my desire to toss them off at that exact moment, I could not fault his logic. After all, his emotional response typically overpowered his logic. The sun began to set again and I, perhaps weakened, decided to offer him a truce should he return. I emptied the bottle of tap water I'd filled with tap water so that he might taste his own death and returned to my position—my legs weary, my stomach empty—waiting for him to return. Waiting for my lover. Waiting for life to return to our nest.

Tosh Berman

Maldoror's Note

Literature belongs to youth. I'm 24, and I can care less about my past or the future. The present is what impresses me the most. I don't have much faith in faith, but love... no, not that either. "Farewell until eternity, where you and I shall not find ourselves together." I wrote letters to her, but I feel a great sense of regret as soon as I drop them off in the mailbox. Since I know where she lives and is close to my home, I would arrive at her doorstep just as the mailman is approaching the door. He would hand me over the mail, and as soon as he disappears around the corner, I would take my letter and leave the rest in front of her door.

Poetry is not about regretting the loss of love but the combination of elements thrown into a cocktail mix shaken but not stirred. The love I have known has continuously been stirred but not shaken. This shall change. "Oh, if only instead of being a hell, the universe had been an immense anus!" Hell, and perhaps Heaven would have been shitted out and join the Earth as it becomes compost for the flies and any other plague-like disease. But, instead, my beloved travels everywhere except to me. She would even go to a far-fetched 1970s shopping mall than being seen with me in a four-star French restaurant. Vanity takes me to a higher form of life, yet, the beloved one travels into the gutter as if it was a fast highway to get to nowhere.

Prose poem or poetic fiction never sits well with me. To be defined by others is unthinkable, but it is unbearable when one puts their own restraints on themselves. To come upon such a horrific relationship is truly "as beautiful as the chance encounter of a sewing machine and an umbrella on an operating table." The either/or of the system at work is not suitable for my temperament. I like to see literature as wide and deep as the ocean. To be on the tip of land and look out into the indefinite space of an endless sea is the closest to bliss. "I hail you, old ocean! Old ocean, you are the symbol of identity: always equal unto yourself. In essence, you never change, and if somewhere your waves are enraged, farther off in some other zone, they are in the most complete calm. You are not like a man — who stops in the street to see two bulldogs seize each other by the scruff of the neck but does not stop when a funeral passes. Man who in the morning is affable and in the evening ill-humored. Who laughs today and weeps tomorrow. I hail you, old ocean!"

I was born in Uruguay, my Pa was a French consular officer, and my mother was dead by the time I was four or five. I remember her in the shadows. Even now, I feel disgusted that I fed off her breast for food. There is something repulsive in obtaining nourishment through another living creature, such as a mother. When she died, I have no memory of pain or even her existence. Except being part of her body in such a manner where I will always feel attached to a presence that won't let me go. I can speak English, but I think in the combination of the languages Spanish and French. I feel my identity is fluid, like liquid dispense in the ocean. One of the great pleasures I had experienced (and still today) is urinating in the sea. Knowing that the DNA or a part of me becomes one of the many elements in the ocean.

As a child, I collected the Spanish edition of the comic book *Aquaman*. How I long to become the king of the underwater kingdom. I wish that my father was a lighthouse keeper and my mother was an Atlantean queen, but in turn, I'm a spirit in a human body. Unable to do things, but only in my imagination. I often feel like Arthur Curry (the human given name for Aquaman), when in fact, my true spiritual sense, I'm Aquaman, King of the Seven Seas. It may not be evident to the light reader, but many of my texts came from old Aquaman tales from the 1950s. The most interesting power he has is the ability to communicate with all sea life. In fact, Aquaman has the power of telepathic control of all aquatic life. His only weakness (if one can call it that) is that he must be in contact with water at least once per hour, or if not, he could die. On that last account, I, too, feel the need to stay as close to a body of water as much as possible.

The only sea life I feel comfortable with are sharks. I actually even fell in love with one. There is something repulsive about their energy and focus only to eat and have sex. Sexually, I identify with the male shark's hunger. I once approached a female shark, and my session with her was one of the greatest

18

pleasures in my life. My disgust for everything and especially for God, I think of this as I reach an orgasm with the shark. Once finished, she left me. For an odd reason, this didn't depress me but gave me a sense of happiness. I regretted my past relationship with the human. I realized that I must never focus on the past but only on the present. Therefore, existence will not be mine, exactly. Still, nevertheless, I do know six songs, and those pieces will exist. "Poetry must be made by all and not by one."

'Stop, turn around, go no further.'
On translating Lautréamont's
The Songs of Maldoror

One of the frustrations, the challenges, the problems – and probably the joys – of translating is choosing the correct idiom to translate into. Taking the words, sentences, phrases, lines, from the language of one country and translating them into the corresponding or equivalent language of another country is the type of work that can be done by almost anyone.

However, choosing the absolutely perfect cultural, social, geographical, spatial, historical, temporal and linguistic framework to put the translated words onto is another matter entirely, and will very much depend on the translator's intentions and the receptive vocabulary of the proposed readership.

And when it's poetic prose, or as in this case, prose-poetry that is being translated, the task becomes even more complicated and the problems suddenly multiply. Should the prose-poetry be translated into a poetic prose equivalent? Or just into poetry? Or prose? Should it be of its time? Or of the translator's time? Or should it be translated for future readers? Should the translator's loyalty be with the original writer? With the intended reader? Both? Neither? Should the translation be accurate? Accurate to what? Or to whom? Should it be faithful? Should it try and convey the original's meaning? The message? Or should the translation try to replicate the 'tone' of the original? Or should it try to be true to the original's 'spirit' – whatever that is?

Having answered all or, as is more likely, none of the above, and using Borges' comment: "The original is unfaithful to the translation" as a mantra to aid concentration, the translator can then proceed.

At the beginning of *Les Chants de Maldoror*, Le Comte de Lautreamont's warning is very clear:

"Il n'est pas bon que tout le monde lise les pages qui vont suivre; quelques-uns seuls savoureront ce fruit amer sans danger... Écoute bien ce que je te dis: dirige tes talons en arrière et non en avant."

These lines are translated as:

"It is not right that everyone read the pages that follow; very few will be able to taste this bitter fruit without danger... Listen to what I say: stop, turn around, go no further."

Immediately it can be seen that, worded in the way it is, Lautréamont's warning to the reader at the beginning of *Les Chants de Maldoror* serves less as a warning and more as an open invitation to the curious; as a none-to-subtle dare; as a direct appeal by a writer to a select few to persevere and read his words.

Over the years, several translators have attempted to translate *Les Chants de Maldoror* from French into English. Lautreamont's 'warning' can now serve as the translation yardstick.

In 1922, John Rodker translated Lautreamont's warning as:

"It is not a good thing for all the world to read the pages which are about to follow; a few only will, without danger, taste this bitter fruit... Listen well to what I say to you: direct your heels backwards and not forwards."

There seems to be deliberate verbosity and vacillation at work: Rodker's reference to the "pages which are about to follow" rather than "pages to follow" or "following pages" is verbose, and adding "and not forwards" to "direct your heels backwards" is unnecessary.

In 1943, Guy Wernham translated that warning as:

"It would not be well that all men should read the pages that are to follow; a few only may savor their bitter fruit without danger... Listen well to what I tell you: set your feet the other way."

The phrase "all men" immediately becomes problematic as

it alienates (possibly deliberately) all other potential readers. The phrase "set your feet the other way" was probably acceptable syntax in 1943, but it sounds archaic and cliched in the twenty-first century.

In 1970, Alexis Lykiard translated the warning as:

> "It would not be good for everyone to read the pages which follow; only the few may relish this bitter fruit without danger... Hear my words well: retrace your steps, do not advance."

The phrases "Only the few may relish" and "hear my words well" suggest that English is not Alexis Lykiard's first language. And 'relish' is an interesting substitute for "taste" or "savor." There is a certain lack of nuance in both phrases that obscures the warning of imminent danger and the simultaneous invitation to continue reading.

In 1978, Paul Knight translated Lautréamont's warning as:

> "It is not right that everyone should read the pages which follow; only a few will be able to savor this bitter fruit with impunity... Listen well to what I say: turn on your heels and go back."

"It is not right" improves on "It would not be good" and "It would not be well," and Knight's use of "impunity" works well. However, "turn on your heels" is a worn-out and hackneyed phrase that ruins the last line by removing the abrupt imperative of "turn around," or of Lykiard's "retrace your steps" or even of Wernham's "set your feet the other way."

As can see be seen, the translator in each case has chosen a specific idiom which the lines have been placed into. "Poetry," as Robert Frost observed, "is what gets lost in translation." In the translating process outlined above, much of the poetry does indeed get lost; it is during the same process that much wonderful poetry gets found. There are, as can be seen in some of the above instances, specific losses and significant poetic gains.

If the translator's task is simply one of trying to capture the era in which the poem was written, which is really a job for historians, then a fairly literal translation is the correct one to try and achieve. If one is trying to bring beautiful old lines of prose-poetry into the present day and retain their beauty and their validity, then a radically different method is required.

One of the real joys of translating prose-poetry and poetic prose is the choice – the huge number of words and phrases available to the translator. There are so many possibilities. It is a very creative medium, for although a translation can only ever be one translation – unless it too is translated, it can be, and often is, one version of many. Poetry is what gets found in translation.

Ultimately, the best way to translate poetry is to read the original, then put it away and write your own.

Douglas Doornbos

Scolding the Hedgehog: On *Maldoror*

Against my better judgement, I told my friend about the book. Prior to our conversation, I had avoided all mention of it, despite how visibly the reading had altered me. But Raymond possessed a soul that resembled mine. To not speak of the book would have betrayed our special bond. So in the morning, at our usual café corner, I risked his disrespect or worse. Against my better judgement, I went on at length about the novel whose title I dared not name above a whisper. Raymond, for his part, sat in a narrow-shouldered silence. The only question he asked was about my physiology. I told him that the changes weren't likely to be permanent. We parted.

Needless to say, the early hours of the night were sticky with regret. As I lay in bed, quietly swelling back into shape, I imagined the concerned messages Raymond was sending to my family or the police. This shifted over time into a wordless dread whose source I looked for in the green membranes of space beyond the ceiling. At last, a luminous squid of thought swam to me. So powerful was the force of its insight, that I sprang immediately from bed and set out, silver lamps swinging in the corners of my vision. The insight was this—everything I had said about the book was wrong, and wrong in the most fruitful of ways.

I had been wrong to tell Raymond I was scandalized by the book. The scandal was my own enjoyment. The scandal was that every time I had encountered a sentence of particular horror, I had chosen to read the next.

I had been wrong to suspect that the dead author's life might have explained or equalled his work. One needed only to picture that drunken god beside the road to see that creations always exceed their creators.

I had been wrong to say that the book held me at an arm's length. For I was the blond soft-eyed child, tortured then saved. I was the mutilated girl and the lecherous dog. I was one of those mysterious brothers racing along the beach. I was the boy on the bench in the Tuileries. I was the man hung from his hair, as well as the witches whipping him. I was accomplice and I was victim. I was Aghone and I was Mervyn, foolishly presuming I'd remain unscathed.

I had been wrong to locate the enigma of the book's hero somewhere in the depths of his character, for all of him *was* on the surface, the very surface of the text. One might even argue he was that surface. What else could sit for thirty years and stay alive, still ride horseback beside its reader? It had no need of sleep, of dreaming. It didn't apologize. It committed its crimes knowingly and would not have done otherwise. It couldn't. One had to picture the scrubbed scrotal sac, the girl smeared across a wall, the velvet cloth the color of soot, the scalped man's scalp, the flayed man's cloak, the black swan on a white page, the foaming face of the ocean—where dorsal fins are but sharpened waves—to understand what I meant. This flatness did not diminish the book's hero to me, for the surface was where all kinds of cuts could occur—cuts of logic, desire, narration. And from those cuts came the blood, pouring out in excess.

Finally, I had been wrong to call the book unique simply because it was strange. What made it unique was what it said to me about all of literature. What it said had already begun to color every title on my shelf. What it said, by extension, had begun to contort my conception of language on the whole. I could see the vast history of our human speech, gushing, pooling, congealing, cresting into waves for a moment before vanishing—all from a small cut, an originating error in the animal. What was it? The change was not Promethean. It wasn't something given, but something taken away. A maladaptation, a mutation, a mistake forming the seed of all subsequent mankind—it was the ability to misunderstand.

It was near morning when I had finished explaining all of this to Raymond. Kneeling down, I looked through the bindings of duct tape and saw that he had still not grasped my insights. Not fully. Granted, he had stopped thrashing about and weeping, but his lily eyelids continued to ebb and flicker with confusion. I refreshed myself with some mineral water from his pantry, cleared my throat, and began to elaborate further . . .

Seb Doubinsky

MONUMENT IN THE SHAPE OF A SEWING MACHINE

O Isidore!
How to exist
After Hugo, Nerval, Baudelaire
And the shattered Rimbaud?
How to dare splatter the walls of poetry
With more bile, more blood, more semen?
How to deface its statue
While fucking it in the arse
With love?
O Isidore!
How to sing the fringe,
The murky depths,
All the circles of hell
Not as ballads
But as an hymn?
How to sing yourself,
Monstrous hybrid
Of youth and centuries,
Longing for lust,
Death and a good laugh?
O Isidore!
The streets of Paris
Are narrow and smelly,
Far away from Montevideo
And its South American ghosts!
More modern the spirits here,
Maybe? Electric? Magnetic?
More French? Educated?
Classy? Stuffed-up?
Bah! Walls are walls,
And borders are imaginary.
Only imagination is real
And the desire to write.
O Isidore!
Breaker of porcelain plates
Some call poetry,

Crashing the party
Some call academia,
You rocked the boat
Until it sank and you with it.
Corps et biens, as they say in French,
Which means your body was never found.
O Isidore!
Buried nowhere, missed by no one,
You shine still like the beautiful
Sewing-machine presented in a shop window,
Your ghost holding a spunk-stained umbrella,
You shine from the darkness of the deep
We sometimes call Life
Or Art
Or Literature
Or Poetry
Or whatever

Steve Finbow

The Art of Appropriation – Stealing Books in the 1970s

On Sunday 16th May 1976, I stood in the crowd at the Round-house, Chalk Farm, to watch Patti Smith and her Band. They were supported by the Stranglers; I have never liked them. A year earlier, I had bought *Horses* and rushed home to play it to my friends. We loved it and it became part of our canon along with David Bowie's music from *Space Oddity* through to *Station to Station*, the New York Dolls, the Stooges, and whatever nascent punk rock there was from both sides of the Atlantic. And because I had bought and listened to *Horses* and read the interviews with Patti, I had discovered Arthur Rimbaud and then Charles Baudelaire and Stéphane Mallarmé and, coincidentally, through a school teacher, had also become infatuated with Surrealism and Antonin Artaud and Hans Bellmer and Max Ernst and Victor Brauner. There was really only one bookshop in London that sold books on these subjects and that was Compendium Books in Camden Town. And so, as a teenager, I would take the train to Richmond and then the old North London Line to Camden with my rich girl-friend and she would buy me books. I still have *Arthur Rimbaud Complete Works, Selected Letters* translated by Wallace Fowlie from 1976. But, for some reason, despite the (un)natural mélange of Rimbaud, Baudelaire and Isidore Ducasse, Comte de Lautréamont, I had yet to read Lautréamont's *Les Chants de Maldoror* or *Poésies*. Abandon incredulity: that will please me.

About eighteen months later, I was working backstage at Richmond Theatre, mostly in the flies. Being in the flies with up to six other fliers was like working on a pirate ship – it was dark, noisy, smelly, ropes everywhere, cleats to tie them off when bringing in or letting down a backdrop. Some were so heavy they required four of us to bring them in and out. It was also dangerous. A trapdoor at one end opened onto a rickety metal ladder that stretched down to the stage. "Trap open" needed to be called when someone entered or exited – a couple of people had been severely injured falling through the open trap. Before I got to work, or during a break if we were working Saturday matinees, I would either go to the pub, the Cobwebs was closest, or, if we had a longer break, the Old Ship for macaroni cheese, a sausage and a pint of London Pride. Sometimes, I would scour the bookshops for something to read on my next visit to the pub. I was reading a lot of Samuel Beckett and slowly plodding through Marcel Proust – minimalism/maximalism – and had started to read the *Collected Works of Antonin Artaud* published by Calder. But I could never find Lautréamont. I do not wish to be decried as a poseur. I shall leave no memoirs.

I need to say here that I rarely bought the books in question, I was very adept at stealing them. I would buy the odd book just to maintain the trust and friendliness of the bookseller. At first, the shop I stole books from – new and second-hand – was W & A Houben Booksellers in Church Court, Richmond, close to the Angel & Crown, another favourite pub. And then one day, I ventured further – not much further, around the church and across the road from Artichoke Walk – where I discovered the Richmond Bookshop. There were three aisles with floor-to-ceiling bookshelves. The place was claustrophobic and full of books on literature, art, history, politics – a lot were academic volumes but there was a treasure trove of remaindered and second-hand books. The place was staffed usually by John Prescott (not that one) and sometimes by students. Mr Prescott could have been a precursor for Driff Field, the (legendary / infamous / imaginary) bookdealer who appears in Iain Sinclair's *White Chappell, Scarlet Tracings* and Chris Petit's documentary *The Cardinal And The Corpse*. Criticism must attack the form but never the content of your ideas, your sentences. Act accordingly.

During one of my many visits, I discovered two volumes of the Artaud *Collected Works*, a volume of Jean Arp's *Collected French Writings* also published by Calder and there on an eye-height shelf the recently published *Lautréamont's Poésies* (Allison & Busby), translated by Alexis Lykiard. I couldn't steal all four and I didn't want to have to hump the nearly 600 pages of Arp around after work, so I decided to buy *Poésies* and enquire about *Maldoror* – it must have been payday. I could appropriate the Artaud another time. I can't remember how much it was but I paid the money and asked my question. Prescott was gruff and not particularly keen on having a post-punk in his shop and he mumbled something and I left with the book. But I had a problem. I knew that Lautréamont had written *Poésies* after *Les Chants de Maldoror* and in it had refuted the earlier work and swapped moralism for Maldoror's immoralism. As a teenage post-punk, I wanted to read the immoral words before they were refuted. In my bedroom, I put the book on the shelf that contained Friedrich Nietzsche's *Beyond Good and Evil, Thus Spoke Zarathustra, The Will to Power*, Thames & Hudson's World of Art editions of *Surrealism* and *Surrealist Art* and Andre Breton's *What is Surrealism? Selected Writings, Andre Breton and the First Principles of Surrealism* and *The Manifestoes of Surrealism*, purchased (the security was strict) on a couple of visits to the Dada and Surrealism Reviewed exhibition at the Hayward Gallery sometime between January and March of that year. Youth listens to the advice of its elders. It has unlimited confidence in itself.

But my tastes were changing. I no longer considered myself a punk, I was a post-punk – New Romanticism was still in its embryonic stage. I could no longer listen to the Pistols or the Clash, my tastes had become darker, I preferred – much to my friends' horror and amusement – Pere Ubu, Cabaret Voltaire, Suicide. Beckett and Proust had been replaced by Yukio Mishima and Jean Genet, the leather jacket swapped for a long overcoat and the spiked hair by a floppy fringe. I had gone all the way to Lewisham to see The Fall and would later that year go to Uxbridge to watch Joy Division. Once it has become a maxim, its perfection rejects the evidence of a transformation.

A life-changing event occurred at the Riverside Studios, Hammersmith, one night between the 11th and 23rd of April 1978. My friend Gary and I went to see Shuji Terayama's *Directions to Servants* performed by the Tenjō Sajiki underground theatre troupe. This was a type of experimental theatre I had never witnessed before. Taking Jonathan Swift's satirical essay as a base, moving it through their stage laboratory of gesture, noise music, costume and live and wriggling koi – it was like Chinese opera on acid, speed and cocaine. I was transfixed. Towards the end of the piece there are four scenes – 16: Anybody Can Be a Master, 17: The Eve, 18: Shoot the Southern Cross, 19: Absence, followed by the stage direction – "These four scenes, which include improvisations, demolish the storyline that has developed thus far. The world that has been dominated by the absence of a Master suddenly splits open, to reveal an inner hell." This show seemed to pull together everything I was interested in – Artaud's Theatre of Cruelty, the Theatre of the Absurd, Mishima, industrial music, sadomasochism – and place it in front of me as a spectacle. Nothing which is true is false; nothing which is false is true. All is the contrary of dream, of illusion.

Back at work at the theatre, in my imagination, I invented an English version of Tenjō Sajiki – but what literature could be used to act as a script? I returned to the Richmond Bookshop and received a begrudging nod and grunt from Mr Prescott. I walked around the shop to the shelves which held the French literature. And there it was – Lautréamont's Maldoror, translated by Alexis Lykiard and published by Allison & Busby in 1970. I opened the book, skipped to the opening lines... "May it please heaven that the reader, emboldened, and become momentarily as fierce as what he reads, find without loss of bearings a wild and abrupt way across the desolate swamps of these sombre, poison-filled pages. For unless he brings to his reading a rigorous logic and mental application at least tough enough to balance his distrust, the deadly issues of this book will lap up his soul as water does sugar. It would not be good for everyone to read the pages which follow; only the few may relish this bitter fruit without danger. So, timid soul, before further penetration of such uncharted steppes, retrace your steps, do not advance."

A cold shiver ascended my spine. It was like seeing Max Ernst's Celebes and Men Shall Know Nothing of This for the first time in a gallery. Later that year, I would get a similar feeling on first playing D.o.A: The Third and Final Report of Throbbing Gristle. I flicked through the pages and recognised passages of proto-surrealism, anarchism, antireligion, sadomasochism, nihilism and horror. I went to the counter and stopped myself thanking Mr Prescott for finding me a copy. He put the book in a paper bag and mumbled something. I paid him and walked across the road to St Mary Magdalene's churchyard where I sat and read a few more pages. One can only judge the beauty of life by the beauty of death.

In the following weeks, I made plans to create a theatre piece based on Les Chants de Maldoror and Edgar Allen Poe's "The Tell-Tale Heart" – I no longer remember why I had decided this was going to be an experimental gothic-horror mash-up – maybe Poe's opening lines... "True! --nervous --very, very dreadfully nervous I had been and am; but why will you say that I am mad? The disease had sharpened my senses --not destroyed --not dulled them. Above all was the sense of hearing acute. I heard all things in the heaven and in the earth. I heard many things in hell. How, then, am I mad? Hearken! and observe how healthily --how calmly I can tell you the whole story."

The nest week, I stole a copy of *The Black Arts*, edited by Richard Cavendish and published by Picador Books, this was to be my stage manual. I drafted in friends to be actors, other friends to be stagehands, other friends to provide the music. I would write and direct and design and paint the stage sets for it. Over the next few weeks, everybody else lost interest and said they would rather go to the pub or to gigs than listen to me prattle on about Isidore Ducasse, Comte de bloody Lautréamont. And so the book was never made into an experimental theatre piece, or, at least, not by me. And soon the shock of Maldoror began to fade once I had discovered William S. Burroughs's *The Wild Boys* and J. G. Ballard's *The Atrocity Exhibition* and Kathy Acker's *Kathy Goes to Haiti*, all of which I had bought (not stolen) from Compendium. However, none of these books would exist without Lautréamont's *Les Chants de Maldoror* and Ducasse's *Poésies*. In fact, the work of Burroughs, Acker and even my own (non-)writing derive from the anti-morality of *Maldoror* and the philosophy of appropriation embedded in *Poésies*. "Who speaks here of appropriation? Let it be known that man, by his multiple and complex nature, is not unaware of the means of extending its frontiers; he lives in the water, like the hippocamp; flies through the higher layers of the air, like the osprey; burrows in the earth, like the mole, the woodlouse, and the sublime maggot."

I no longer steal books, just the words inside them.

Faisal Khan

PELICAN

Among the catalog of animals, the pelican, whose image is given not without the distinction between animal and man: the pelican offers its own flesh to its young, a 'love as would shame men.'

Faisal Khan

Infinite Enigma

Be so good as to look at my mouth
        Maldoror, Fifth Canto

- Imagine the most efficient of machines. Perfectly calibrated in all respects. One with not one particular function, rather all conceivable functions. A machine of universal utility. A machine functioning too as its own corrective: a machine that is its own technician.

- Consider the reception of this book over the years:

- Adulation: Breton, who spoke of the shedding of all shackles; Artaud, who called Lautreamont the most lucid of geniuses.

- Benjamin, Cesaire, both of whom spoke of the book's insurrectionary nature.

- William T. Vollmann, one among those artists who remind us that it is indeed possible for the greats to be still here and working even in this age, alive and walking among us: "Lautreamont taught me how important and how possible it was to write a sentence that is gorgeous." Vollmann himself, like Lautreamont, testament to that very importance and possibility.

- By others he is written off as a mere madman.

- If any social function could be attributed to art, that activity considered by too many to be ultimately useless, by others commodified in the most crass manner, then consider art as therapy: Gentileschi's Judith, therapeutic art par excellence.

- Consider the words of Cioran, kin spirit to Maldoror and fellow insomniac, who said that a "book is a suicide postponed."

- (Therapy allays. Holds off.)

- The Romanian who, like his contemporary Beckett (an other practitioner of black humor), shed his native tongue to write in French, who pursued the elusive ideal tongue, who dreamed of "a language whose words, like fists, would shatter jaws."

- (How close to this language is the language of the Cantos?)

- And yet another practitioner of black humor and fellow literary enigma, boring through life and consciousness via language to what lies beyond, yet one who failed at properly erasing himself (as Ducasse so beautifully did: no original manuscript, a death not even described, no corpse) that jackdaw from Prague, who said: "I am a memory come alive, hence the insomnia."

- The insomnia of the hyper-vigilant.

- Why enigma? Perhaps because he was a relic. Some thing that lived on when everything like it had died out. One among those that worked deep in the belly of the cave, in the dark against the wall. Those "technicians of the sacred," as Mircea Eliade called them, that were, through their own will or not (though who is it that would willingly have themselves flayed alive?) are purged through a series of rites, given gifts of sight, are then born anew. Was he among those shamans, born outside his time?

- Is this an art we know of today? The art Bataille speaks of in his book on the ancient art on cave walls? Com modified, commercialized, categorized as "art" now is?

- With that conception of art in mind, would it not be true to say that *Maldoror*, especially with its unpalatably dark humor, is something that cannot be com modified, hence necessarily obscure? What canon would contain it? In which syllabus would we find this book? Where would this be "required reading?"

- This is a literature that knows exactly what it is doing. An ever-vigilant literature. All commentary and criticism built into its very structure. A literature that knows itself to be guilty, that knows and acknowledges its origins.

- Consider Bolano, admirer too of Lautreamont. Is not *2666* steeped in the Lautreamontian spirit? A book, of our own time, that, like *Maldoror*, turns Literature inside out. Destroys it from within. Illuminates its pretensions.

- And the breathless narrator of By Night in Chile, who considers the origins of literature.

- (Is it not the torture chamber where literature is born? Is it not in abjection?)

- Go as far back as the first known written poetry, that of the ancient Mesopotamian priestess Enheduanna, poetry written during a time of dread, uncertainty, turmoil. Is it not calamity and disaster that has proven, over and over, to be the ground from which the greatest literature springs forth?

- As shaman one must go *through* the pain, as if through a corridor, unlit but for its beginning and end, no up or down, no right or left, nothing to distract oneself from the pain, only the wall to lean on in the worst moments, only beginning, to which one cannot return, and end, the arrival at which, and subsequent release, is not guaranteed.

- (The shaman's katabasis. The descent of Inanna and so many before and after her.)

- The shaman's survival never guaranteed.

- (This one is gone while barely beyond adolescence.)

- No memoirs. No such self-indulgence.

- Is this the removal of the *I*? The self-erasure of the mystics?

- Ibn Abbad: "Then the self is only ashes."

- (Lautreamont: "I know that my annihilation will be complete.")

- The mystics can trace their own lineage to the shamans. There are two experiences of mystical obliteration: one in which one becomes, after the purging, whole, coherent.

- The other experience is one of complete annihilation.
- "...both throw up their arms."

- Nothing before. Nothing beyond. Clipped life.

- Necessarily incomplete.

- ("No further information.")

- But you had wanted to read of evil? To sit in your comfortable armchair, at your leisure, and read of the sufferings of others? Well then. Here you are.

- This is not literature at all. But an evisceration of literature. A knife's blade cutting it open up its center.

- Le Clézio from his essay "The Freedom to Dream": "Dreams are the hidden fire that man must steal off with in order to reveal the other side of himself, in order to attain real freedom."

- Is the fullest reality that of the dream? That phenomenon that we relegate to oblivion upon awakening. Our age knows nothing of this freedom, we have destroyed the nocturnal, we want nothing other than to be surrounded by light. We have assumed that true creative birth comes with light. But perhaps not. Perhaps its origins can only be infernal, born in the dark.

- Upon the initial reading there comes a time when you fling the book clear across the room in horror, or disgust. Why do you pick it up again? Because through contemplation, a contemplation that must necessarily come when one is thoroughly disturbed by something, you see that that very reaction is exactly what the author intended. You hear his laughter.

- Perhaps no enigma at all. Perhaps what this work calls for, as Sontag suggests (with respect to art in general), is an undoing of the mystification, to look at this work and take it for what it is, just as we would take the Song of Songs for the erotic song of love and pro found longing that it is, prior to any interpretation.

- (What is it then? What is *Maldoror* prior to any interpretation?)

- Regard it soberly.

- Aimé Cesaire, *Discourses on Colonialism* (Monthly Review Press, 2001): "Monstrosity? Literary meteorite? Delirium of a sick imagination? Come now, how convenient it is![...] Lautreamont had only to look the iron man forged by capitalist society squarely in the eye to perceive the monster, the everyday monster, his hero."

- And Lykiard suggests that Lautreamont is not to be approached with excessive reverence and adulation (which Lautreamont is already anticipating and mocking before the reader even acknowledges it themselves), nor is he to be dismissed glibly (as if the explosiveness of *Maldoror*, in pure aesthetic terms, were some fluke of a madman's feverish imagination).

- It would perhaps not be a stretch to say that all readers have felt one or the other sentiment, that they have, for the most part, occupied a pole, an extreme, for at least a moment. Indifference for one who has *read* the text is difficult to imagine (again: what canon would contain this book that one would feel obliged to go through the motions of reading it, like an automaton, as we read much of what is given to us as "necessary reading": the works of the zeitgeist, the "greatest books ever written," "what every reader should read before they die"?

- What we can do then is to take the work for what it

most certainly and unequivocally is: the manifestation of an undeniable talent, one who was, despite his youth, a true practitioner of dark humor, tearing down all established things, and a true technician of language, the steady fall of this smith's hammer being heard each time we open the book, wielding language like a blade.

- Consider the Argentine angel, Alejandra Pizarnik. The last lines of a poem written on a chalkboard, found in her studio after her suicide: "I want to go / nowhere if not / down into the depths // oh life / oh language / oh Isidore"

- Language juxtaposed with Isidore? Yes, without a doubt. But life? Why not? What is life but pure freedom?

- And one final time, K. His final written entry in his diaries. He too held strong and fast to that blade:

- "More and more fearful as I write. It is understandable. Every word, twisted in the hands of the spirits – this twist of the hand is their characteristic gesture – becomes a spear turned against the speaker. Most especially a remark like this. And so ad infinitum. The only consolation would be: it happens whether you like or no. And what you like is of infinitesimally little help. More than consolation is: You too have weapons."

Faisal Khan

Maldoror

...the fact is, I was not laughing.
      Maldoror, First Canto

An image of our hero is made difficult by the sheer abundance of his metamorphoses. He is never static, never still, nor is his form. We can imagine only glimpses, glimpses that quickly fly off just as soon as our gaze stretches its hand forth. Here, the ruined mouth. His failed attempt at a laugh, made with a blade, from the corners of his mouth outward.

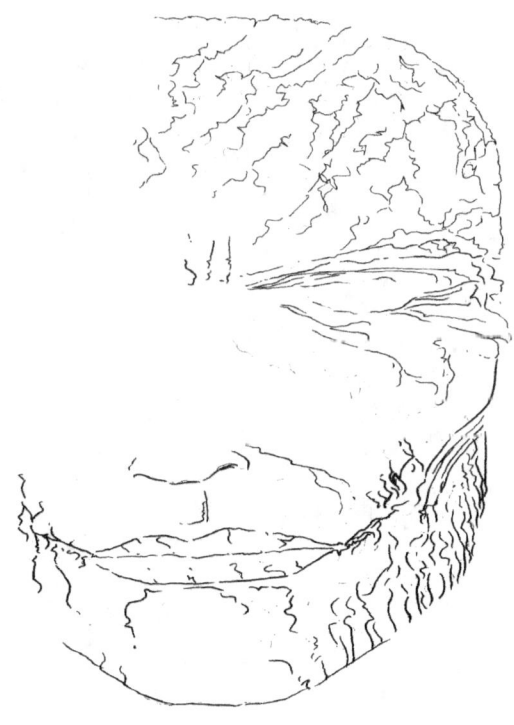

Faisal Khan

Shark

I sought a soul that might resemble mine...
Maldoror, Second Canto

Among the dense mass of episodes and images: the shark.
Our hero drawn toward her, having watched from far off her
appetite, an appetite much like our hero's own.

Dylan Krieger
Three Poems

the hierophant hosts a dinner party

everything is almost ready: hell is in the oven
heaven halved and gutted
the tradition is to feel nothing, but he can't help it
the illuminati of the colorless earth are all here
business-faced, unlistening, with their backs to the machine
whatever they're eating sports an undercarriage like an insect
instead of grace, they say something later redacted, later erased
the last course is served on a need-to-know basis
wriggling, red-pink, still alive at the center
uncanny, how blood sacrifice changes shape but never goes away
the circle of satellite orbit and the circle of the headless chicken
intersect like a corporate logo
street artists reimagine it as testicles or tits, of course
and for all we know, that's what it stands for
for all we know, the meaning of life is to bone

belief in evil

when you believe in evil, steaks don't taste right
the lilacs collapse under the weight of dumbstruck fungus
little girls still hide from bright lights in the park after dark
new crop tops snagged in brambles but half repaired down the
block
nobody's watching, until you don't want it—then they're everywhere
resewing the flowers and asking what happened
so you say evil, beware of dog, a bad man is easy to find
and all the aftermath nods knowingly, like it's normal for escape
to feel as narrow as the throat mid-swallow, mid-throwup
people who believe in evil tend to believe it lives here
in the gut, with the rest of the engines we've forgotten
how to take apart—parasitic, sick with secrets, past quick fixing
at dusk now, we lock the doors to shut it out, but it doesn't work
i don't believe in evil, and if i did, i have already worn it thin

the rest of history

i walk around with no underwear or curtains when i want attention
spot a neighbor at the iron-wrought gate of my nightmare and
wave

whoever stares back long enough turns crystal into powder into
pressed pill
hypnosis doesn't work unless you're already down the drowsy spi-
ral

hunt inside yourself--gunshot for breakfast, shoreless swim out at
night
unprotected sex with strangers whose faces filter the city into a
mirror ball

i remember your names, like the rest of history, only because they
are written down
neatly organized in temporal order with annotations on context,
optional patronymics

i lie wide awake, pretend i am sleeping prey, and survey those who
strike:
what is the taste of the meat you miss most? the backseat, the attic,
twisted

hand-hold over the banister--i insist you're sentimental when you
do it
follow the sound of your own fangs piercing my empty fists without
argument

in the lavender half-light, i'm thinking of all this when i see you
through the window
before dawn, when it's still too dark to notice, and you don't look
up, not once

Callum Leckie

**Two Portraits of Isidore Ducasse/
Comte de Lautréamont**

Alexis Lykiard

THE UNMENTIONABLE

They owe it nothing yet they fear it
Lautréamont

As well described by Ducasse and John Donne,
a Presence reigns whose bite is nowhere fun.
Of that most intimate, undaunted parasite
none but the brave must ever dare make light.

Through these gigantic leaps that thrill the mind,
it lives like God – as teasing, hard to find.
Beyond good or evil, here is what best exists,
deflates correctness, proves itself, persists.

It prompts urgent debate, lends a fine sensual itch
to metaphysics and relationships, on which
the greatest lovers with their cats agree:
nothing defeats the perennial flea.

Chris Lloyd

Reflections on a Piece of Music Not Yet Written: *Maldoror*, the opera

I first came across the magic of *Maldoror* on a whimsical journey through Montmartre, Paris, in a scenario bordering on cliché during a *psychogeographic dérive* that led me to the small Espace Dalí– a wonderful little gallery tucked away behind the Sacré-Cœur, whose collection focuses less on the artist's well-known paintings, and more on his sculptures, sketches, and illustrations.

Like many others, it was through Dalí that I was introduced to *Maldoror*; which feels exactly how Philippe Soupault and André Breton would have wanted it upon rediscovering this self-published ode to surrealist madness. At the time, I was working with an interdisciplinary group of scientists and artists, and we were seeking inspiration for our next work, after spending a year exploring multisensory pairings between food, wine, and classical music.

The permanent exhibition at the Espace Dalí contains copies of several works that were either inspired by music or literature – the interdisciplinarity of it all piquing my creative intrigue. In the collection were Dali's drawings for the *Tristan und Isolde* opera (composed by Richard Wagner), Shakespeare's *Romeo and Juliet* (which was arranged into the famous ballet by Sergei Prokofiev), *Alice in Wonderland* (realised by multiple composers) – and tucked away, almost daring to be discovered: *Les Chants de Maldoror.*

Being a veritable cultural luddite with extremely limited language skills, I came to the quick assumption that the *Songs of Maldoror* must either already have been a piece of music, or else some form of strophic text that could support a new song cycle. An idea was borne: a concert experience designed around Dalí's artworks, combining the literature that inspired the works, performed in counterpoint with music deriving from the same source – potentially with a new work based on this new discovery. Simple.

Needless to say, life is never that easy; for whatever reason this concept never took off and the idea was placed back on the parochial shelf for a few years. But *Maldoror*, like any true love, retained his place in the periphery of my mind, for both the potent potential and mysterious mysticism its pages promised to contain. I cannot remember exactly where or when it was that I finally found my beloved - and now worn out - copy[1] , but I can clearly remember the palpable excitement experienced when I finally found myself gorging on its content that very first time.

It was one of those rare moments when your expectations are not only fulfilled, but exceeded. Akin to the first time one hears a masterpiece like Brahms' *Piano Trio Op.8*, or Stravinsky's *Rite of Spring* in the flesh: the recognition that you are glimpsing into greatness; the concurrent appreciation of savouring something new that you know you will return to – whilst understanding the need to appreciate this first experience, because you will never get to relive your exact feelings and responses in the same way again.

 Of course, I'm writing to an appreciative audience who can probably relate to these exact sentiments in their own way; though perhaps a unique aspect of my first acquaintance with *Maldoror* was the ongoing fascination I had with its content being realised in musical form.

Eventually, I approached an opera director and composer about the potential of working this text into a new opera composition – one that would represent musically, visually, and aesthetically the imagery Lautréamont/Ducasse paints so vividly. Our librettist took one look at the work and said it would never work.

The composer and I planned a week in London to debate the merits of the work, spending hours every day sitting opposite each other at a table in a bedsit in North London discussing the philosophy of new music composition, the role of opera in the 21st century, and the arguments for and against reimagining an historic European work that glorified misanthropy and violence, in preference of contemporary narratives that told the stories of underrepresented, diverse societies. I would argue that the sadistic and sociopathic figure at the centre of our story was as contemporaneously relevant as it was at first press (this was in 2017, in that wonderfully dystopic cluster-

[1] Thanks eternal must be given to Mr. Alexis Lykiard for his phenomenal translation; and the Exact Change publishers for the layout and presentation of the book that communicate aesthetically what the words portray.
[2] #OperaHarmony was a project curated and produced by Ella Marchment in 2020 during the first wave of Covid-19.[1]

fuck of a season that saw Brexit, Trumpism, Le Pen, Putin, al Assad, Erdogan et al take centre-stage) - his retort being that it wasn't necessary to look backwards to find examples of systemic crises that can be challenged through art.

By the end of the week, the project was yet again placed back on the shelf – relegated to the status of something that should exist, but for whatever reason, cannot, for now.
But then, an email arrived.

An email that poked at the smouldering coals; one that rummaged at the back of the closet where things lay near-forgotten: an invitation to participate in an anthology collection devoted to the 175th anniversary of our once-forgotten, now-revered, dearly departed author, Isidore Ducasse.

I sent a screenshot of the email to the opera director, Ella Marchment, with the simple caption: '#memories'. Which was soon followed by a WhatsApp conversation which read:

Chris: "We should do it
           Ooooh idea
           Not a through-composed opera, but vignettes
           Different composers
           OPERAHARMONY2021?!?"
Ella: "OMG LETS"

And yet again, *Maldoror* has reared his sometimes ugly, sometimes beautiful, sometimes sharklike features to be a figure of inspiration: how will it turn out? Will we finally hear the world that Lautréamont depicted? Can a staged musical work ever capture the exquisite combination of cruelty and beauty, mixed with a healthy dose of absurdist tragedy? I believe so, though surrealism has been notoriously difficult to depict musically – as opposed to other 20th century movements such as Impressionism or Expressionism. According to composer Dr Evan Kassof:

"The problem is, is that surrealism is predicated on absolute meanings being dissolved, [for instance] with the automatic writing style, where it's like 'we have words, but are they really words? Or do they mean what we're saying?' And music starts from a point of abstraction, so you can't abstract it into surrealism." [3]

Attempts have been made by artists far greater than ourselves; even the effervescent Erik Satie was unable to truly

---

[3] Interview with the author, 23.5.2021

succeed in musically portraying the surreal (though his 1917 opera *Parade* in collaboration with Picasso, Diaghilev, and Cocteau was a solid attempt at a precursor). But to surrender now would be to give in before all attempts to explore the material have been exhausted. Maybe the musical interpretation requires going deeper than the purely surrealistic nature of the text and looking further into the psychology of fear, or the philosophy of the sublime; perhaps it is in the creation of an entirely new theatrical-musical performance concept. At this point we promise this: we will try and fail as many times as we can in the hope of realising this vision – and if we come to the conclusion that futility is our only option, then I am sure each reader will agree, the existence of *Maldoror* on paper is more than enough inspiration for one lifetime.

One thing is certain: *Maldoror* has sunk his fortnight-long fingernails into our creative minds, and he will not relinquish his grip until we have exhausted every opportunity to realise its musical potential.

Jennifer MacBain-Stephens
The Best Authors

The Best Authors

               endowed

annex esteem from poetry

men with   obscure   problems
    grapple the satanic

and frayed sailors

you devils

spew forth   your victims' brains

on the planet   they inhabit

worm ridden paintings   of   geometry
                     dreams

lips: an air pump sucking out   every   turn   on   the
                wheel of life

     in arguments I hope to leave in one piece

one maniacal roarer devoured his wife

years ago

         her mother's milk   dry

the best authors   celebrate   in   blood

Christopher Nelms

Melinda Gates and Ghislaine Maxwell at Bluebeard's Castle

For Lautréamont

Twilight my way back from pitted hearths
we come to the ruins of Tiffauges,
fed by the powdered bones of youth,
buggered, massacred, and burned.

At the dark horizon of other hills
an orchard shadowy and grim
the place they sought not in the bottom
where The Egg lifted the gaping yawn
of its gutted flank, but on a hill

where light already held them spitted
overlooking the creek, the glades and muck.
On this place where we are usurpers,
yesterday's mushrooms, the meds are helping

which is *"so good to hear."*
The wind blew the prophylactic from our home,
but what can we do? We are not mistakes.
Sometimes we are stuck in them,

very attached to understand more
about an event, us a receipt saying,
"I want out being part of something."
I do not know what this is.

It may be too simple.
Whatever it is, it's true.
It's not self-service.
Kill me and you'll never find out
In shy boredom's hour hate's thy house,
Supperless, raging, under saddle all day
Long heedless of underbrush or log
I grow fast as a dog;

I don't want to know
Where I came from, I
Want to know
Go right now
To become a great
Empty marriage to witch

The sky is connected
By a clear black pastel

Even meaningless
Frustration preferred.

Golnoosh Nour and Chris Kelso

Ça Fais Mal

Sisyphus

Joe tosses a coin to the counter,

Let's it spin until it loses energy in the absence of friction

And schlepps his shopping over one shoulder, his good one

Allows himself a superficial glance at the Auschwitz tattoo on the clerks forearm

Before he leaves with a *ding ding*

His good shoulder aches under the stress of the shopping-bag-weight

The Spica is twisted too tight, see

Joe's bad shoulder, which aches too

He let it get that way, amen

Pop an analgesic, let the heavy bag falls by his leg

Let the shopping tumble to the floor – a six-pack, more analgesic, some tape.

The drugs, a real miracle of ingenuity

On his knees in the street as each vertebrae crack in sequence

The phone rings

He lets himself answer it

A man on the other line with two good shoulders

Joe watches as his shopping rolls into oncoming traffic

Allegations from a
Jagged sun-scar mouth
I hide from it, from your spotlight
Shadow is a home of mine
Soft envelope of ink
A place where you can leave behind
The stress and strain, the need to constantly THINK, THINK,
THINK
A place to lose the need to please the blinking, scabbed sun
Shadow is a friend of mine
You can whisper your secrets into its abyss
Not like you, when I talk
When I TRY, TRY, TRY
To block you out as best I can
I've been burned before by your hideous red planet

When you ask me about the
world outside?

    I don't want your judgement

I pray for amnesia everyday

    I just want the dark

But your face is impressed upon
my mind

    A sooty comfort blanket of
    forgetfulness

Twist my brain into a hangman's
knot

    Because, really, who wants to be
    reminded all the time?

I'll stop learning new things

    Confabulation, I'll re-remember
    events to suit me

Keep the suns at bay

    I can't remember the president's
    name

Solution:
Let the Darkness Speak

Listen! I am the son of Filth. I obeyed Mother, and inherited an instinctive and extreme cruelty that has made me all the more angelic. I am convinced by evil and you will thrive, you will become a star in the starless sky if you take my advice:

Conceal your darkness from the masses, not me. Let me hook my claws into the scabs on your scurvy nape. Let us relish my criminal oil, let my moonbeams make the tomb's marble gleam, I am a radiant angel, my magnificent palace is built of silver walls, golden columns and diamond doors. Worship my pernicious presence, for I, with my angel's wings, with my sinful intensity, only I know how your sins put us in the most virtuous situation. Sanction the sadness, inject the joy that comes with sucking, sticking anything into anything, absorption of skin, anything sacrilegious anything sick and sardonic is sacred to me, for I am the one who sniff the ashes of past lovers, I who murdered my shame in the sea, I am sand and I am sane, I grow darkness within me. You might cut my tongue, but I have sharp teeth and shark sex, my allure is in – inside you already – and in vincible. I burst into fits of laughter like a hyena, I received life like a wound, so I kiss the sea, weeping, for I defied death and divine vengeance with a supreme howl, I am on the dark side of my selves, of your selves, my slave (s), say my name – a ritualistic prayer in a horror game. Take my advice, and you will be wickeder than I! I am the idol that breaks itself, I am the

sin that slaughters himself, I am
the soil that stains herself, I am
the dark celebration of your

virtuous lover's death. I am the
glorious collapse of an empire in
decay, I am the sin, the scenery,
the sacrilege, the only rule, and
rupture.

I shall break you

and you

will beg

for it.

Jeremy Reed

If Francis Bacon had Painted Isidore Ducasse

Isidore, my nineties novel that attempted a fictional recreation of Isidore Ducasse's mutable sexual ambiguity, and attracted film potential from Derek Jarman, who was at the time stripped by HIV into an emaciated, partially blind dead man walking, like everything written on Ducasse was subordinate to lack of substantiated biographical data, denied historic exponential by the author's gated secrecy and attempted immolation of identity by adopting the pseudonym Lautréamont, the intransigently iconoclastic author of *Maldoror*.

There's what, other than a few surviving letters, and a bleached uncharacterised likeness of him provided sixty years after his death by his school friend Paul Lespes, a scratchy imputed and highly disputed photo of Ducasse sized 9.2 X 5cm, circa 1867, of Isidore at Place Maubourquet, Tarbes, discovered uncaptioned in a photo-album of the Dazet family, Ducasse's guardians, by Jean-Jacques Lefrere, and a number of addresses at which he lived, including 23 Rue Notre-Dames-des-Victoires, and in 1869, transitioning between 32 Rue Faubourg-Montmartre to 15 Rue Vivienne to 7 Rue du Faubourg, Montmartre, as the hotel in which he died aged 24, on 24 November, 1870, at 8am, and a death certificate that specifies no cause of death, suggesting he died without ever having lived as some freak agency of a-causality.

Google Lautréamont and his occupation is given as poet.

What Ducasse didn't lack was money. He was it seems provided a generous allowance by his father Francoise Ducasse, a French consular officer in Montevideo, Uruguay, where Isidore was born, and was able to self-publish anonymously the First Canto of *Les Chants de Maldoror* in 1868, and additionally to finance the total of six cantos published during late 1869 by Albert Lacroix in Brussels, who feared to distribute the book for reasons of being prosecuted for blasphemy and obscenity.

Ducasse's acute absence, impenetrability, and the lack of fixed historicism in the figure of the author lend him like Rimbaud to a drifting culture of destabilised personalities who without precedent create and violently abandon the work they have created. There are books that appear to arrive like aliens out of the future, and to have no direct relationship to the past, and *Maldoror* belongs to this strain, as does the intensely hallucinated agency of Rimbaud's *A Season In Hell*, the morphic autonomy of Breton and Soupault's *The Magnetic Fields*, the cut-up of William Burroughs' smacked out *Naked Lunch*, or the collaged post-apocalyptic iconography of JG Ballard's *The Atrocity Exhibition*, as examples of the radically subversive properties of unrestricted imagination at war with consensus reality.

Haunting's a subterranean activity and Ducasse spooks the reader because the text has no identifiable or relatable source. *Maldoror*, as a book, remains like an unsolved crime, its unanalysable pathologies forcing the reader into observing his or her potentialities to do the same. Nobody can read *Maldoror* seriously without becoming an internal accomplice to the atrocities committed by the protagonist. If books bleed, then this one does.

It's impossible to write about the dead, and particularly the enigma of Isidore Ducasse without of course implicating one's own subjectivities as to who he was independent of his fictional creation Maldoror, and perhaps the very opposite of the psychotic chimera liberated by his unconscious as the locus of implicit knowledge into imagined form.

That Francis Bacon never painted Ducasse was a serious omission in his assemblage of distorted biomorphs in which the body was violated to figurative effacement by the aggressive brushwork of an excoriated portraiture that is like *Les Chants de Maldoror* without any direct precedent in singularity. Near the end of his life, when I would periodically meet with Bacon in a subterranean bar at Piccadilly Circus, we talked of extreme episodes in *Maldoror*, a book he knew, like the anti-hero copulating with a shark, but more of its youthful creator's limitless neural plasticity, and his possible suicide, murder, or death from plague, as states suited to the crisis in Bacon's art of radically deforming facial recognition into a collapsed morphology of physical extremes.

The little, and detail-inadequate that we know of Ducasse's physical appearance originates from his old school friend Paul Lespes, who interviewed by Francois Alicot for Mercure de France, 1 January 1928, disclosed: "I knew Ducasse at the Pau lycee in 1864. He was with Minivielle and me in the fifth form, and in the same study. I can see him now, a tall thin young man, slightly round-shouldered, with a pale complexion, long hair falling across his forehead, his voice shrill. There was nothing attractive in his features."

This underexposed description seems to radically contradict the photographic image purporting to be Ducasse, in which the young man's prominently large forehead, the short dark hairline receding a long way back, suggests little of the long-haired person remembered by Lespes, whose description is as generalised as that of his publisher Leon Genonceaux, who described Ducasse as 'a large, dark-haired young man, clean shaven, mercurial temperament, neatly dressed and industrious.' The latter characterises someone who could have been anyone. No eye-colour given, no detail of the mouth, no hairstyle, no suggestion of introspective mood, or imperatively, his psychological disposition. We are left with another absence, as though Ducasse eluded composite biography by having adopted the alias Comte de Lautreamont, as the name that would travel with his book *Maldoror*, like a forged passport through history. Even his death certificate (no. 2028) wasn't signed by a doctor, but by the hotel proprietor J.F. Dupuis and A. Milleret, one of his staff, with no cause of death given (sans autres renseignements). Did they in fact, murder him, it being at the time the Siege of Paris, in which the invading Prussians attempted to starve, freeze and demoralise the city into submission. As Paris became increasingly squeezed for resources, exotic animals from the zoo were served in the best restaurants, rats sold in Les Halles, while the city's marauding poor raided cemeteries for fresh bodies to cook and eat.

In my imagined Bacon portrait of Ducasse I see his eviscerated body contorted like a hacked octopus abandoned on a bed under a hanging naked light bulb, the tentacular twist of entrails seeping black ink as spillage of atrocity, a red arrow pointing to a legibly pulverised copy of *Maldoror* on the floor, and the seeping lavender curve of a windowless wall registering as backdrop, as though Ducasse is the victim of homicidal butchery or the unexplained self-motivated explosion of his viscera.

I want to stay with the image of the flayed octopus, as in Canto 2 the adversary of Maldoror sees the latter morph into one: "How violently shocked he was to see Maldoror, changed into an octopus, fasten eight giant tentacles round his body – any of which could easily have circled the planet, and caught off guard struggle against the viscously strangulating grip of suction pads that attempted to squeeze the blood out of his body, before managing to detach himself abruptly to take temporary refuge in a cave."

What Ducasse possessed to unlimited degree was access to the psychic content of intuitively perceived knowledge as a bridge between those processes that Jung called the personal unconscious and the collective unconscious as the re-appropriation of archetypes. It's suggested Ducasse spent a lot of his time in Paris in libraries reading science and illustrated encyclopaedias and books on natural history as a facilitated resource for *Maldoror.* In a method similar to Bacon's accidental retrieval of visual images from a chaotic montage of degraded photos, cut outs and reproduction of images from books littering his studio floor at Reece Mews that were integrated as random signifiers into the sensationalised imagery he exploited, so much of the exaggerated and exotic bestiary that Ducasse appropriates for his text most possibly owed its origins to the illustrative books he consulted in libraries, and manipulated into the disruptively surreal imagery that bleeds into *Maldoror's* relentlessly violent narrative. A lot of what Ducasse wrote must have personally shocked him in the process of writing it and scared him into attributing authorship to his alias Lautréamont in order to dissociate from the book's more toxic pathologies.

Written episodically, the text of *Maldoror* is best read randomly, as Ducasse's reliance on optimised shock and sensation demotes narrative to a secondary role. In a letter dated 23 October 1869, one of the few of his to survive, written to Auguste Poulet-Malassis, the publisher of Baudelaire's notorious *Les Fleurs du Mal*, in the hope he would support and help circulate the book that Albert Lacroix so feared to distribute, Ducasse confessed, "I have written of evil… Naturally I exaggerated its properties in order to create something new in the context of literature that while it propagates despair does so with the intention of the reader reversing the motive to good." But of course that wasn't the intention at all, anarchic subversion of the consensus world was entirely Ducasse's objective, and intuitively aware of psychic upheaval in the turbulent times, he was to write to Poulet-Malassis four days later of his approval of Ernest Naville's lectures on The Problem of Evil, given the previous year at Geneva and Lausanne, as part of "an imperceptible current that goes on expanding," and of how Naville's lectures collected into book form were published in Paris by the bookseller, Cherbuliez, as a book presumably of interest to Ducasse.

Ducasse precedes and resembles the Rimbaud of A Season In Hell, as both commentator and critic of his own text, both simultaneously elevating and deconstructing his motives in writing by obstructing the reader's impartial viewpoint and deliberately preventing flow. This method of continuous counterargument to the emergent text supplies total authorial control over third party involvement. Bacon too, in disrupting all narrative content to his paintings, as an anti-illustrative paradigm, contested "to give the sensation without the boredom of its conveyance." Or again in his conceptual aims, "I know it can be illustrated, I know it can be photographed. But how can this thing be made so that you catch the mystery of appearance within the mystery of the making."

It's a method he would doubtless have applied to his never executed study of the enigma of Isidore Ducasse with a violence of aggressively applied paint corresponding fully to the deviated text of Maldoror with its saturated anarchy of experience.

"I invested my talent in portraying the pleasures derived from cruelty," Ducasse tells us in the First Canto, and he meant it, both the facility to do so, and the commitment to the spectrum of perversions celebrated by Maldoror as personified evil. And Ducasse most certainly wasn't pathologically insane, the myth of him established by Leon Genonceaux, who never actually met him, as someone who wrote only at night, hammering a piano wildly with his fists, while he extemporised the text of Maldoror, is most probably a romantic fiction contrived to establish madness as an apology for the book's concerted assault on received concepts of morality and societal norms. On the contrary, the author's almost schizoid dissociation from the crimes he perpetrates within art, suggests not only his exemption from their actuality, but that the work is imported from some unknowable side of himself with a limitless capacity to violate the ordinary experience. Ducasse's imagination immersed in sex or mutilated death is in the process of writing transferred to Maldoror as the text's transgressive protagonist. You can of course commit limitless crimes in art with no moral accountability other than censorship, and Ducasse far more than Rimbaud, and in this respect much closer to Burroughs pushes authorship into serial criminal activities with a distinct same-sex orientation. Right from the imaginary process of drinking a young boy's blood at the book's outstart, something detailed with a deviated psychopathological twist that differentiates it from prototypical vampire literature, the author commits himself to the dedicated perpetration of imagined atrocities in an art that meets its subject at the mind's limits. And the potential to transfer unconscious phenomena into its actual realisation must at times have scared if not traumatised Ducasse, in the way it probably contributed to Rimbaud's abandonment of literature before he was twenty through the fear of precipitating a toxic symbiosis between the imagined and the real wrestled with in the hallucinated field of *A Season In Hell*. And if we attribute Ducasse's death to suicide, then there's a strong reason to suggest he feared madness, rather than was mad, and that the apologetic publication of two small booklets of Poems, between April and June 1870, as an intended retraction of the corrupt fabric of Maldoror, was also an attempt at therapeutic healing. What he does make clear though is his awareness of the distinction between ideated and real experience. "Communicate to your readers only the experience of suffering, which is not the same as suffering itself." Again, exemption is implicit in Ducasse's refusal to take personal responsibility for the contents of his writing. "Feelings are the most impartial form of reasoning that can be imagined," he suggests, the whole plagiarised methodology of Poems, in themselves not poetry anticipating the sort of disengagement that would have Rimbaud affirm "Je suis une autre," – I am another, as a sort of splitting crucial to a poetry of hallucinated consciousness in which the author is aware of the fissured split.

I want to return again to the idea of a Bacon portrait of a sensationalised Isidore Ducasse, perhaps mutilated by a shark. Bacon was always insistent that he wasn't painting the person representationally, but the associated images characterised by the elusiveness of individual personality in which he manipulated human frame and flesh almost out of recognition. He attributed most of his disruptive image-making to the accident of oil paint: "the medium is so fluid and subtle that every change that is made loses what is already there in the hope of making a fresh gain."

What if this time we revert to the claustrophobic constrictions of a typical Bacon interior, a lurid orange or purple backdrop of the kind used in Henrietta Moraes (*Lying Figure with Hypodermic Syringe*), only this time on a collapsed circular bed we have the mutilated body of a post-coital Ducasse lacerated by the shark he imagined his fictional protagonist fucking in the shallows. What if the trunk of Ducasse's mauled body tapers into that of a shark's suggestive of their convulsive union having taken place not in the sea, but within the confinements of the sealed room in which Bacon invariably isolated his subject. Wouldn't that constitute aspects of a Bacon meta-fiction of the almost no-person, Isidore Ducasse?

The text of *Maldoror* is saturated in morphic shapes that are part human, alien, hybridised, spooked and invariably malevolent in terms of hauntology in its applied surrealist sense. Like Bacon in his approach to the human figure as effaceable agency, in which the images both anticipate and recollect the event that lay beyond the moment they were painted, so Ducasse is obsessed by the concept of deformation of bodies into chimerical phenomena. A whole imagery is hallucinated into a-causal possibilities – a crab is reborn from its resolved atoms, a fishtail takes flight with two albatross wings, and the protean mechanistics of the "Maldorean sea," appear to contain the accumulation of inherited psychic structures and archetypal experiences Jung attributed symbolically to the collective unconscious into which Ducasse seems to have constructed a backdoor into the subliminal potentialities of non-cognitive poetry. In Ducasse, things fall up, rather than down, and although he continually addresses the reader as counterpoint to his authorial viewpoint, the negation of personal detail and everyday life in Paris, again prohibits all access to personal identity, so that we come to assume Maldoror is Lautréamont, but Lautréamont isn't Ducasse.

Anomalously, there is a moving scene in the Second Canto, that one feels was personally witnessed by Ducasse, out and about in Paris, and that is the drowned body of a youth who committed suicide washed up by the Seine, and the attempts to resuscitate his body when it is pulled bloated from the water and attracts the invariable crowd of morbidly fixated rubbernecks. I'm convinced that Ducasse witnessed rather than imagined the incident, as part of the urban abjection common to big cities, and the fact that most poets are by occupational distraction flaneurs. It's a rare occasion when Ducasse occupies a local rather than non-ordinary space in observing a body rolled downriver by the Seine, and the description of the drowned boy seems to come from direct observation, allowing for the sense of despondency that genuinely enters the writing. We feel in this instance that for once Ducasse substitutes for Lautreamont, before the event is quickly subverted into ideated violation of the dead body.

In fact it's only in the final Canto that Ducasse establishes Paris, and a personal appropriation of the Latin Quarter as a physical basis for the work, suggesting the reality that it takes time to internalise knowledge of a city's complex geography and to integrate it as a design into imaginative reality. We're told in the specific detail of mapping a quarter that "Mervyn walks directly from his front door following the Boulevard Sebastopol as far as the Saint-Michel fountain. He takes the Quai des Grands-Augustines and crosses the Quai Conti: the moment he passes the Quai Malaquais he sees on the Quai de Louvre, walking the same way, someone carrying a sack under his arms who seems to be scrutinising him carefully." We feel in the sudden immersion of street signs that Paris is now undeniably the complex physical extension of Ducasse's body won from purposed walks that situate his writing in the urban present.

A sense of Ducasse's environment returns again in the same Canto, when he describes the street in which he was living the rue Vivienne and its shops with their window displays lit up, observing the gold watches in a jeweller's, as stores close for the night. It's 8pm, by the clock on the Bourse, and people are going home, and a woman faints and falls down in the road. Hunger was endemic at the time, and in the context of the narrative, the action again seems real, if incidental. And although the neighbourhood is eclipsed by the malevolent aura of Maldoror as a stalking psychopath, this psychic intrusion is comparatively alleviated by the intricate knowledge of local topology. This is Ducasse's neighbourhood. "On reaching the main road he turns right and crosses the Boulevard Poissonniere and the Boulevard Bonne-Nouvelle. Arrived there, he turns right down the Rue du Faubourg Saint-Denis, leaving behind him the concourse of the Strasbourg railway station and stops in front of a tall gateway leading into Rue Lafayette." He's out walking and observes familiar street names, and again, we feel we have sighted Isidore Ducasse in a rare moment of the ordinary.

What Ducasse and Bacon unconsciously share in common is an anarchic preoccupation with the body as corporeal meat and with its organic functions as the substrate of images that repel by their manipulated exposure as aggressive metaphors for components that are usually concealed organs. Both externalise the internals of their subject with a predatory disgust for anatomy that is absent in Rimbaud who invariably finds beauty in whatever he sets out to destroy, his symbols invariably being associated with colour, right down to designating each vowel its own appropriate colour in the poem "Vowels."

Suggestions of Ducasse's homosexuality like Bacon's graphically identifiable sodomy in paintings like *Two Figures* 1953, influenced by a Muybridge photograph of two wrestlers in combative pose, and painted while the artist lived in a furnished room at 19 Cromwell Road, are of course made corporeally and brutally explicit in flagrantly misogynistic scenes in *Maldoror*, but most forcibly in the defence of homosexuality as Ducasse's most likely sexual orientation. "If only," he writes, "this sad universe was instead a celestial anus – notice the hard-on at my abdomen, I would have rammed my cock through its brutalised sphincter, smashing the walls of its pelvis with my sexual violence, in the process discovering the real subterranean truth of sex, and the unleashed torrents of my viscous sperm have found their true outlet."

Ducasse then goes on to specify that his ideal same-sex partner should be no older than fifteen, and to further the shock impact of his confessions, informs us, "I even murdered a queer recently who didn't live up to my demands. I threw his body into a disused well, and there's no real evidence I did it."

And although Ducasse is committing an imaginary crime, an art homicide, the pathological content of the writing is clearly initialised to fulfil his own deviated fantasies as he would have been only too well aware that not only would his book have no readership, but realistically invite prosecution for obscenity if it was circulated.

Was suicide perhaps the only way Isidore Ducasse could split with Lautréamont? From 1962, until his death thirty years later, Francis Bacon took the prescribed anti-psychotic Librium on a daily basis, together with a cocktail of antidepressant and anxiolytic drugs to help manage the ontological assault of his renewed creativity each day in the accumulatively littered debris of his oxidised Reece Mews studio. It was his way of containing the overreach of potentially psychotic phenomena. How Ducasse negotiated the precarious frontiers of imagined and real we'll never know, as the impudent affront with which he condones atrocity is doubtless more literary artefact than unconscionable transgression.

Maldoror as a one-off explosive was a hard book to own to by the enigmatic Isidore Ducasse, and must have appeared to its author on completion an endpoint rather than a start. He seems in Paris to have formed no durable friendships, no relationships that we know of, no contact with other writers, who like Rimbaud he ridiculed for their careerist reticence, and consigned his book to the accident of being retrieved in the future. The day after his death on 25 November 1870, he was after a service at the church of Notre-Dame-de-Lorette buried in a temporary grave in the 35th section of the Cimetiere du Nord, from which on the 29 January 1871 his body was exhumed and buried in still another temporary grave in the 49th section of the same cemetery, in land built over by the City of Paris in 1879.

What would Bacon have made of Ducasse's death if he'd resituated it in the excruciating centrality with which he isolated his figurative images? Would the room with its characteristically spherical curving wall have been painted a neutral Dulux primrose, and would the contorted body as remains trying to escape its boundaries have by implication been sexually aggressed by Maldoror as its internalised psychic occupant?

Plague, suicide or murder? The choice is yours, and the answer unknowable. The book *Maldoror* still travels through time as an exceptional anomaly that probably wouldn't have surprised Ducasse, but I'm making the error of thinking for him. Suicide was morally taboo at the time of his death, but what other way would he have wanted? Like Rimbaud he'd said everything too young to warrant a future in writing, and lacked any readership or possibility of contemporary under-standing. Ducasse was too far ahead of his times to return from the future. He'd done it all on the page, and perhaps death was the only renewable option for adventure.

John Reed
Disruptionary, or Contrabulary[4]
Nine Preliminary Entries (in alphabetical order)

Afterlikes
noun
AF·ter·lahyks
The immediate feeling, after many likes, of unfulfillment. Example: "I posted this video of my cat and got crazy hearts—and then I had *afterlikes* so bad I ate two tubs of rocky road."

Agitblah
noun
AJ·it·blah
Art/literature with an agenda that's obvious, one-dimensional, stupid, or boring. Example: "The movie offered proof and assurance that all we need to colonize Mars is grit and duct tape."

Censorcorum
noun
sen·sor·KOHR·uhm
Censorship through taste/decorum. Example: "Yes, there were rats spilling out of the kitchen, but it just wouldn't do to talk about them."

Corprogressive, corprogressivism
adjective, noun
KOR·pruh·greh·suhv
Action by which corporations or similar deflect responsibility, impede change, or implement a self-serving agenda by espousing a progressive position, which may be laudatory in and of itself. Example: "The speaker, a celebrated environmental architect, will discuss the benefits of the 'honeycomb' office layout." *Corprogressive* ideas are often put forth by "patsy" experts who knowingly or unknowingly advocate for corporate positions. The term may also designate individuals: "Seven corprogressives attended the weaponless weapons think tank."

---

[4] After Gustave Flaubert's Dictionary of Received Ideas, and Comte de Lautréamont's Poésies

Evolutionary Recession
noun
eh·vuh·LOO·shuh·nehr·ee ri·SESH·uhn
The premise that money/inheritance is an impediment to evolution; i.e. through inheritance, cycles of generations are excused from evolutionary pressures. Example: "Herman's grandfather, with hard work, brains and brawn, amassed a great fortune; Herman's father lived for foxhunting; Herman, unable to do or want to do anything, wasted away in a semi-vegetative state." *Evolutionary recession* may manifest in deficiencies of intelligence, sanity and/or socialization/education/competence.

Fish-eye, fish-eyed
verb, noun
FISH·ahy, FISH·ahyde
To overestimate one's own importance in relation to others. Example: "Nobody even knows who that dude is, and he thinks his competition is Ben Affleck? What a *fish-eyed* fool."

Flipsider
noun
FLIP·sayhd·or
One who believes that with a certain level of success, creative freedom or virtuosity can be attained. Example: "Once I'm an influencer, I can make my music, and give it out for free." Example: "He thinks he can work his way to the top of the fur trade and get everyone to go faux."

Oswaldorator
noun
OZ·wahl·dor·aa·tor
A speaker or participating attendant who is unaware of his/her/their contextual agenda. Example: "Once again, Johnny Potato Chip, for no ulterior motive he could discern, was granted a complimentary pass to the soft drink convention, where he wandered the floor, giving out free barbecue potato chips to each and all."

Simplexity
noun
sim-PLEK-si-tee
Complicating something simple through workflow or process. Example: "Hold on, I have to type in dates, fix spelling errors, and input points of origin and estimated prices in this

grocery list app."

The Case of Arthur Craven, Solved

Mexico, 1918. Arthur Cravan, poet and boxer, pugilist and ponce, stood in shattered pink crab shells and chains of creaking green weed, appraising the car hood ocean flatly lain out and clanging beyond the concave shawl of the bay— cliffs at his dorsal spine, blue-gray vistas ahead. The boxer's spine was a helical vessel concealing many aliases. His uncle was the sissy Oscar Wilde. Cravan wore only his sealskin trunks, a hunting knife grinning from the waistband. He had the agreeable sensation that all of the thousand egos that he had forged within himself were coming to an end—the message centre was overwhelmed, drowning like a brain under punches— A whitewashed skiff was pitched in the gravel of the beach.

> With increasing emotion, I kill myself
> Through pleasure.
> I die of love, in the gills of one
> Of the sharks.
> Life has no solution, tall fins, a sharp
> Blade in sun.
> Always I carry with me a steel
> Voluptuousness
> Like Jack Johnson.

Another figure, Isidore Ducasse, had been born in Montevideo—not far away—and stood now upon the gull-scat promontory above the beach. Ducasse wrapped himself in a black leather trench coat, his jet lustred mane fingering across his porcelain complexion, thin bones—riding boots bearing the spermatazoic residues of space travel. Flickering between dimensions of death, he watched Cravan hauling the pale skiff into the water, rowing with his back to the waves—manta ray flap of his muscles. Ducasse began to assemble his rifle, his ruby lipstick making his pout heavy, sipping absinthe from a silver flask—sun on the nineteen-inch biceps of the rower—a hard groin—Jack Isidore is a character in the Philip K. Dick novel *Confessions of a Crap Artist*. Jack Isidore says: "We don't feel at home anywhere we go."

> Creeplight stains the ziggurat
> Ball courts of abandoned skulls
> In Quetzalcoatl's hollow jungle.
> Cochineal husks in the musks
> Of the aftergame and the grave.
> Quixotic picadors dulled by Cortez and
> Cactus spines lacklustre within
> The killing irons.
> Quiere llover.
> ¿Quieres darme ese libro?
> ¿Quieres un helado?
> Cravan turns his back on everything.

Arthur Cravan watched the recession of the land—memories of snake feathers—savouring the weight of the oars, and observing with a wry smile the saltwater that seeped into the boat. The hole that he had drilled through the wood possessed the perfect dimensions, like an hourglass for the ocean. Soon, he would be far out, and the vessel would be sinking as he had planned. He would complete his stunt, and swim ashore—another casual dare to himself, an examination of his flesh and ego. There was no place for art in the modern world. The sinews beneath the tanned skin of his forearms were more poetry than most could muster—The skin stretched across his spine—As the boat filled with crystals and began to capsize, he knew what he must do. He took his hunting knife and carved a shallow gash across his abdomen, watching a thin curtain of his blood run into the lunging brine. Rolling overboard, he kicked away from the boat and began the return swim to the bay. His limbs thrashed into the surface, churning with purpose a pink scum in the water. They would come for him soon.

> What is this army of sea-monsters
> cleaving the water so rapidly?
> There are six of them; their fins
> are strong and they are forcing their
> way through the heaving seas...
> Blood mixes with water, and the water and
> the water mixes with the blood.
> Their wild eyes light up well enough
> the sea of carnage...
> With increasing emotion, such as he has

never felt, the spectator follows this
new kind of naval battle from the shore.
He no longer wavers, he shoulders his rifle.
-Maldoror; 2:13. Isidore Ducasse.

The spectator in lipstick gazed upon a carnal vortex imploding one hundred yards from the promontory, his heart spliced with admiration and sorrow. The swimmer had split out the guts of all six of the sharks. Now, he was ripping their silver rocket faces with his knife, stabbing at eye jelly and their exposed gums as they tried in death to bite, once more. The swimmer himself was torn and bloodied, his left shoulder was dislocated—shreds of livid muscle hung off the creamy bone—raw meat suspended in red wine—a poet crawling from the flesh vat sea with scars and brags. Yet, the malevolence of Isidore Ducasse flickered down his rifle like St. Elmo's fire. He regarded Cravan's triumphant smile, as he neared the sedimentary shelf of the shore. When, at last, Ducasse saw him rise, as though he might walk the remainder of the way out of the surf, he shot him through the back, shattering his spine and spilling aliases into the carrion broth. Arthur Cravan fell sideward, slowly, and died. Isidore Ducasse watched his corpse float away.

David Leo Rice

On Seediness, Undead Literature, and *Maldoror* in the 2020s

As I pause to take stock of where America stands, or where I stand in America, in the summer of 2021, notions of seediness and decadence fill my mind like spirits drifting out of closets whose doors have long since rotted away. I'm no expert on Lautréamont, but *Maldoror*'s world of omnipresent decay, shot through with dark enchantment and explosive violence, resonates with the ideas I've been churning through this year, as the defining narratives of the past era—Trump and Covid foremost among them—begin to recede, and a pregnant silence stretches out into the future.

The fundamental question that I'm chewing over now, as, it would seem Lautréamont was as well, is whether, in times of ominous lull rather than active crisis, the world decays into chaos, or into a system of underlying horror. Is nature ultimately entropic in the sense that, without human-made order, it falls apart, or is it fundamentally structured such that, beneath any apparent disorder, we are actually in the grip of systems far too vast and intractable to comprehend? In the summer of 2021, without a galvanizing master narrative and—for the first time in five years—without an avatar to project our fear and loathing onto, we are perhaps uniquely able to see the seediness of America for what it is, and to decide, each for ourselves or together as a culture, what to do with what we find.

While the crises of climate change, inequality, and the overall fraying of the social fabric clearly haven't been averted, the summer of 2021, compared to that of 2020, is a quieter, stranger time, one less given to outright panic and more to the kind of creepy brooding that pervades the febrile nightscapes of *Maldoror*. When I was a teenager, I used to like lingering over breakfast for as long as possible, reveling in the feeling of risking being late for school. I called this state "malingering," unaware, until much later, that the word actually means pretending to be sick. Both *Maldoror* and summer 2021 share this aura of malignant lingering, of simultaneously longing for and fearing the future, and thus, in the meantime, lingering in the present to the point of sickness, as if all the freaks and monsters in Lautréamont's work were slow-moving entities waiting to crowd in upon anyone who waits in one place too long.

For now, as we slowly regroup after the paranoid mania of the past five years, the clarity we both long for and fear feels out of reach. We've become hypersensitized—in a state of exhaustingly high alert—but also deadened, numbed, partly asleep. Scrolling Twitter and bingeing podcasts, we've been bombarded by a constant churn of dire news, while also sedated by the consistency of the feed, exhausted by an addictive quest for information that we know can never provide the resolution we've been made to crave. Over the course of the past era—which we're now either emerging from or plunging even deeper into—the world became both insanely over-described and ever less known, putting us in a state where we've seen and read so much about what's going on that we are almost totally incapable of engaging with it in real time and space—we can't even be sure that it's going on at all. It's as if we've been dosed with a hallucinogen and, in our desperation to find an antidote, have resorted to taking more of what dosed us. If that doesn't sound like the condition of *Maldoror*'s narrator, not to mention its reader, then nothing does.

The hallucinogenic feed, which is endless by design, preys on and perverts our innate hunger for meaningful narrative, for a story that evolves toward a valid ending, even as, in reality, it only perpetuates itself. If there's anything to be learned from works like *Maldoror*, and from seedy art in general, it's to develop a better means of remaining in the present, sickened but undeterred, as we attempt to revel in rather than resist the vectors of unrealized futurity that clog every moment with confusion about where we are and what that means about where we're going.

Over the course of the lockdown last year, I explored these notions in a series of essays, where I tried to work out a definition for what I called the *Unworkable Equilibrium (UE)*: a kind of permanent crisis wherein we're both terrified and bored at the same time, poisoned by a psychodrama from which we cannot disengage, even while our engagement is driven by distraction (though we never quite know from *what*). Turning this framework toward *Maldoror* now, I see parallels in the perversions of its narrator, as he attempts to summon, kill, and copulate with *everything all at once*, outside of time, just as the narrative breaks with linear structure and sometimes even with sense itself, to create a new style that torments the mind's sense-making faculties into a kind of masochistic submission, as in a nightmare where all the vague anxieties of waking life reappear in distorted yet horribly tangible form.

By this logic, each bombshell news cycle is a seed that fails to sprout, a momentary jolt that appears poised to bring the psychodrama to a definitive climax and yet, instead, merely gives way to the next bombshell, which in turn gives way to the next, in what becomes a mockery of narrative, flooding the present moment with more and more unsprouted narrative seeds. Failing to sprout into a coherent future, these seeds instead give birth to a monstrous present.

These seeds that fail to sprout are indicative of a larger seedy condition, a stagnant, swampy state that America has fallen into in the new millennium. This stagnation is the rotting corpse of anticipated progress, of the future that never came and thereby revealed that the past, which seemed to be leading to that future, wasn't ever what we thought it was. It can't be a coincidence that I have, along with so many other writers and artists who grew up in the 80s and 90s, moved into a surrealist headspace in the new millennium, attempting to capture the present with an array of monstrous and symbolic forms, just as Lautréamont did in his own moment. Rather than a rejection of reality, this approach seems like the only viable means of even trying to apprehend it.

Day-to-day, we're living in the ever-more-cluttered arena of these unexploded bombshells, while, historically, we're coming to terms with the possibility that we reached a culmination point at the end of the Cold War, when I was born, and yet this culmination was itself either a pseudo-event, or the prelude to an event that still hasn't occurred. While we wait— ever uncertain if there's anything we're waiting *for*—we feel something gigantic rotting deep within the American imaginary, sending up bubbles without yet revealing its nature. As a friend put it last fall, "It's like Moby-Dick, the embodiment of 19th century American ambition at its most ferocious, is now dead and decomposing underwater."

There was thus something gothic about the decade between 2010 and 2020, when my aesthetic sensibility was coming into focus, an aura of old expectations dying off and beginning to rot, without turning the ground fertile enough for anything new to sprout. This isn't the world that the 90s raised my generation to expect, but given that it's the world we've inherited, the art and literature of previous gothic ages can and must form a grounding education in how to navigate this terrain by incorporating rather than rejecting seediness. Perhaps, indeed, this is the only fruition those seeds can attain, so that, paradoxically, the seediest work also goes the farthest toward relieving the seedy condition that engendered it.

Therefore, what I wonder now is whether seediness can be redeemed as a positive value, a sense of still-untapped potential, and thus a way out of the feed that has trapped us in a narrative dead end. Perhaps it can be a means of using the specifics of this moment as pathways into the mythic—the momentary disturbances of the daily news as points of access to an underlying strangeness truly worthy of our attention, a means of contacting the rotting corpse itself, not just the bubbles that break the swamp's surface. As in *Maldoror*, the question is whether we can use the nightmarish specifics of the present as pathways into a unified and eternal nightmare realm.

My thoughts on seediness as a defining American category began to develop ten years ago, when I was fresh out of college, wandering New York City with my childhood best friend. These thoughts grew out of what we saw around us, the cheap fanciness of the gentrifying neighborhoods and the feeling that some major era of history, in which perhaps the *Real New York* had existed, was over, and that we were in the early days of another—though whether this new era would take on distinct characteristics or define itself simply as *the era after all eras* remained to be seen. Perhaps Lautreamont felt the same way as he wandered a version of Paris that likewise seemed to be after everything, a ghost city in which the last vestiges of the real were dead but never quite buried underfoot.

My friend and I were in that transitional phase where we no longer saw ourselves as students, but didn't yet have any purchase in the outside world, nor any non-ironic sense of what it meant to be citizens of a flawed but still extant nation. We were novices in the religious use of the term, absorbing as much film, music, and literature as we possibly could, and, just as importantly, letting ourselves feel, for the first time, what it meant to be anonymous adults at large in a city, wandering day and night without full-time jobs, families, or any other stabilizing obligations. We were, in other words, part of the seediness we saw, or thought we saw, all around us, just as *Maldoror*, in his sadistic manner, is as well.

The essence of seediness, we decided, is the presence of untapped potential. Seediness could be the relic of something that had died and begun to rot, in the sense of a city or a civilization *gone to seed*, or it could be seed that had never had the chance to sprout, in the sense of *spilled seed*, and all the queasy images that such a term brings to mind—deeply American images of motels, truck stops, traveling salesmen, peep booths, the forgotten corners of Vegas and New Orleans, and the dark streets just beside and behind Times Square and Hollywood Boulevard. The queasiness of spilled seed, rather than the wholesomeness of, say, a new pregnancy, calls to mind the fear that this seed has either been intentionally squandered, or that it was unable to take root due to some environmental blight. It calls up the American anxiety of our supposedly super-fertile New World not being what it claimed to be, populated by millions who have remained in a liminal, unsettled state, generation after generation.

The seedy is impersonal, an anonymous layer of human sediment—used sheets, used towels, dirty mattresses, dollar bills. The seedy trace that's left behind when a drifter leaves a motel, and as *Maldoror* passes from one episode to another, is reduced to a patina of past human presence, so that the seedy both erases the human and offers the possibility of its renewal. Rather than starting a new life, the seedy offers the chance to be reborn in one's own life, or perhaps to be born in earnest for the first time, well into middle age. The impersonal nature of seedy motels makes them prime sites for reinventions of this sort—the odds of checking in as one person, under one name, and checking out as someone else are far higher than, say, undergoing the same transition in a Hilton or a Marriott.

Furthermore, the seedy is distinct from the *sketchy* and the *sleazy* in that the sketchy and the sleazy describe a person or place with a definite, unsavory goal—usually sex or money. The sketchy or sleazy operation has already reached its potential, whereas the seedy is both unsettling and alluring because it points to something as yet unknown, a possibility that, like the famous meeting between Harmony Korine and Larry Clark in Tompkins Square Park, might blossom into a genuine site of new culture (before succumbing to gentrification—another form of sleaze—as is the fate of all seedy people and places that overplay their hands). This is another reason why seediness is time-limited, a window of possibility that can't remain open forever.

The sketchy and the sleazy are therefore also deceitful and underhanded—a sleazy cop, a sleazy politician, a sleazy strip club owner—whereas the seedy is more nebulous, more passive, almost mystical, pointing to a possibility that can only be activated by the observer. For this reason, the seedy need not be good or bad, but rather can become either depending on where it leads and whom it speaks to, just as *Maldoror* is an evil character who has nevertheless stirred a positive, pro-creative sensibility in the hearts and minds of readers across two centuries.

Lastly, and most importantly, the seedy is distinct from the *shitty* because the shitty has lost all potential to generate life—the ground in a truly shitty place is poisoned, forever or until some major, unexpected change occurs. Unlike the shitty, the seedy offers something other than repulsion, horror and disgust. There is a value to it that makes it worth discussing here. This is why a drifter holes up in a seedy room, waiting for a phone call, a meeting, or some other means of crossing the threshold into a new chapter of his or her life. It's why, I think, I haven't yet considered leaving America, despite knowing that I may soon wish I had. I'm holed up here, invested in whatever happens, along with more than three hundred million others. One does not likewise hole up somewhere shitty—one gets stuck there, usually by birth, and tries one's best to get away.

This condition of seediness, once my friend and I had come to understand it, frightened and intrigued us in equal measure. It made us feel like prospectors in a Western, though one in which there was no more land or gold for the taking, or like detectives in an unsolvable mystery, where whatever was unknown would remain that way forever. The blinding facades of Best Westerns and Waffle Houses, as we drove around the country, seemed to conceal clues, yet it would never be known what these clues were pointing toward, nor whether the feeling that they were clues at all had to do with them, or only with us.

Therefore, the real question is what avenues out of the seedy and into the mythic are still possible? How did Lautréamont transcend the seediness of his own era to make contact with the horrific but galvanizing nightmare realm beyond or deep within it? How did he transmute his condition into Art, and how can we?

The first step is to begin considering literature undead. It died in the apocalypse of the Internet's combination of news and entertainment, and the inevitable deadening of our ability to resist the resulting feed. This is dispiriting, but it also carries a profound opportunity: if we accept these realities about literature in 2021, we can move with this acceptance into a new era, in which fiction exists for new reasons, thriving within new networks. If we are living in a zombie era, there is nothing keeping us from deriving occult empowerment by becoming zombie authors, embracing rather than trying (and failing) to resist zombification.

This is where I want to fight to keep my attention now: on the undead possibilities of this ancient, reborn art form, insofar as it is still capable of both responding and contributing to the moment we occupy. My deepest creative goal in the early 2020s is thus to find a means of feeling gratitude for the fact that I am still conscious, and that, if I try hard enough, I can choose what to invest my consciousness in. I can try to write and read books that condense and crystallize the ambient strangeness in the air, reaffirming my sense that somewhere, on some level, it does all add up—just never in the ways or places we imagine.

At the same time, I know now that consciousness is also a liability, an asset that can easily be squandered, or stolen by those who seek only to sell it off. We've all learned something valuable from the Internet over the past five years: that our attention is commodifiable, a stock future that can be bought and sold with great precision. We've learned that none of us are as autonomous as we'd imagined, and that our attention is not fully our own—now, as in Lautréamont's time, the air is thick with dark enchantment.

If we emerge from this revelation with a new awareness about who and what we really are, we have an opportunity to move forward. The purpose of undead literature is contradictory on the surface, as it seeks both to respond to the political upsets of the moment, and to refute them by digging back into its own inherent fictiveness. Fusing these two apparently contradictory tasks is the essential literary challenge of the 2020s— to be aware of what's happening, but to use that awareness to penetrate the zeitgeist and make contact with what's hidden behind it.

If we take up this mantle now, I believe that literature will prove still up to the challenge, which is why it has died but never decomposed as an art form. This is the clarifying distinction between the undead and the stagnant: one has passed through the cataclysm of its own demise and emerged into a spooky, exciting territory on the far side, while the other has stopped partway, unable or unwilling to see the process through. Therefore, let us by all means catch our breath and gather our wits in the summer of 2021, but let's not stop here too long, for a full panoply of gruesome and odious beings smells blood, and is on our trail already.

Audrey Szasz

MEDUSA PHASE

FATA MORGANA: "There's no question in my mind," she says — eyes more fascinating than — mean and vindictive, savours of ridicule — every shimmering waveform — hastening youth — let the smoke return to the flame — too fond of the black uniform to relinquish it in this way — unruly seas crash down below — all her unhappiness and female resentment — I smiled politely through precipitous tears — in the middle of nowhere — my frostbitten vulva — crossing the equator — here there are many sirens; but there is no image of them — plaintively lifting the hem of my gingham dress, I begged her for another guitar lesson — a reef half a mile from here — a thousand supplications — used to tattoo the skin with ink made of a dark paste of coconut ash mixed with salt and fresh water — they do not bury their dead; they let the bodies hang from their huts until the flesh has decomposed, then wash the skeletons in the sea — I can make out the handcuffs — my mistress — her mother tongue — a man waiting at the station either fell or was pushed — his blood and internal organs smeared across the tracks — they would never love each other as they had loved each other before — flower garlands, bunches of grapes and vine leaves, marmoreal glances, roseate blush — naked girls on the layered divan — full of hollows — siphonophorae — the remotest islands awaiting landfall.

SPENT PASSIONS & FOUR MORE WISHES: We left the perspiring software developers far behind, taking a treetop walkway and pausing to rouge my nipples before languidly descending towards a ground-level boardwalk that wound around some ancient arboreal behemoths, some of which resembled something out of a Grimm's fairy tale. I was stark naked beneath a transparent Alice-in-Wonderland dress fashioned from ivory lace with a high collar and delicately puffed sleeves. Very coquettish. You held my hand as if to prevent me from straying. Several hours later we learned that the software developers from Silicon Valley and their young families had been slaughtered with machetes by several vengeful tribesmen on the 'sleeping platform' where they had set up camp less than forty-eight hours before. How were they to know that the shelf-like promontory was sacred to the indigenous population? Oh how we laughed. We sipped exotic cocktails, venerating the giant trees, granite ranges and the deserted white-sand beaches. The limitless banality disguised as order and efficiency that these tedious philistines had attempted to impose had been summarily destroyed in the service of my demonic matriarch. Micro-iniquities soon became deliciously apparent; corpses buried up to their necks in volcanic sand. I envisioned myself as perpetually on the wrong end of a Faustian pact. *But that's only self-pity talking*, you chided me. I had always been a supersensual girl drifting through a 'pataphysical world.

SLOANE EPSTEIN'S LAST DANCE: Not wishing to break character or risk the ruin of my alter ego, I refused to submit to the identity scan — their most important tool is made of wild almond wood and sharpened turtle shell — jellyfish arrive at beaches in warmer seasons — many of those who tried to escape cared little about reprisals and were prepared to try their luck — two hundred thousand heavy machines penetrated their juvenile flesh like amorous swordfish — it is by no means agreeable or comforting to find oneself beset by an angry mob of anti-intellectuals hell-bent on ravishing an array of both animate and inanimate child substitutes — be they animal, vegetable or mineral — "I don't want anything but the most expensive orthodontic treatments," I pouted, maintaining the slightly stunted habitus of an insatiable brat, and opened up an occult folio consisting of irregularly sized cartographic sheets with a brief descriptive text for each — all I needed was to traverse the Styx and be skinned and filleted in the attempt — Sloane Epstein was my name — in the play, in this theatre of pain — oneiric agent of marine relations — I meticulously cleaned my braces with activated charcoal toothpaste — we hunted the mysterious Maldoror down and prevented him from destroying all of his charts — once the most diabolical being ever to strut across the surface of this tortuous realm, he had been reduced to a doddering amnesic relic of his former self — according to his idiosyncratic logic, sans map, the terra would remain incognita — seconds before we detained him he was loading up his Winnebago with the intention of vanishing from these obscure parts — we marvelled at his extensive collection of striated infant skulls — *there's nothing situate under heaven's eye — but hath his bound in earth, in sea, in sky —*

LOST IN THE LACANIAN MIRROR STAGE: The patterns are strictly prescribed — they are applied singly or repeatedly: straight and curved lines from which feathered details grow — tearing them to pieces, knocking them about, killing them with axes; it was gruesome — *où suis-je?* — the unwonted and the unwanted — she bombards these shores with feu d'artifice — a barbaric explosion of opaline bouquets — baroque, gilded — zaftig — azure nazars — makes me feel like I'm melting — here, at the outermost edge of the desolate archipelago — *blind, inane, inevitable mass suicide for humanity* — white-collar automatons boxing the Jesuit — making use of the dry-mouthed widow — they were groping for nacreous trout in a quite peculiar river — they were swinging the dolphin all afternoon long — skipping through fleeting shadows, shallow affect — lacklustre — magnanimous pragmatism — *she's a truly charming girl*, the woman said, grabbing me by my shoulders and pushing me towards the guests — *she will turbocharge the imagination of anyone staring over the side of a zinnia-red boat at an infinity of waves that could conceal just about anything* — I promised to serve as a sort of emotional valet or stochastic chambermaid — but my enthusiasm fizzled out on the lower reaches of the moraine — minus my .38 calibre handgun, a prepossessing Colt Python to which I was much attached — shrouded in darkness, they abandoned me to the mercies of nature — her magnetised hemispheres — taste of arousal —

AVE MARIA, S. 558 + MY PINK ZITHER: I lashed the rods together to form the cross; it made me feel like an odd sort of pénitente — we dined on roots, berries, and seaweed, hunted game with spears and snares, dressing in the finest belle époque fabrics and enduring the bitterest winters. I experienced recurrent and troubling dreams involving gangland-style executions. I took advantage of some overwhelmingly crude comforts. *C'est la vie, c'est la mer, mes amis, avant l'affair....* How jejune. That's about my level. Don't worry about it. I won't. *Char de marde.* Where can a girl run *to* in a place like this? Dawn flashed its brilliant headlamps across the barricades. I thought about many things that night; about all the love slaves in unwitting chastity, and old Gloucester's eyes being gouged out; a little blonde boy screaming in agony, his arm torn out of its socket by some rogue chimpanzee — the magic of Kinder Surprise™ — a fun day out at the zoo for all concerned. *If your god doesn't exist, why doesn't he let bad things happen?* Plagues of unnameable creatures and tantalising swarm attacks — whisper your vows — threading myself through the bars of my cage — ineluctably insinuating a poisonous embrace — devil's fingers — succulent species — I deflate your tyres — slash open your face — *strike one!* — scar your sinuous flesh — rendered ravishingly jealous — she took me to a bar in Mayfair where we paid around £100 for a couple of cocktails — the souls of the dead journey to the west, where Nei Karamakuna, the therianthropic woman with a bird's head, blocks the way and demands her favourite food: the patterns in their skin — she ravenously pecks the ink out of their limbs and their faces with her mighty luminous beak. ♫ *When I die and they lay me to rest, I'm gonna go to the place that's the best* ♫

BIEN ENTENDU ~ TONIGHT'S LOW: Beguiled by invidious glamour, their underworld exerts an almost destructive attraction upon me. Darkness helped my inhibitions scatter; in losing my innocence, I entered into the eternal mythos of something unrespectable. Shrouded in warm neons, and so full of an irrepressible sensation of an immediate forever, we gave in to retrograde introspection lying between accretions of disintegrating shipwrecks, our stomachs ripped open and our insides unceremoniously torn out. I entertained a vision of an opportunistically carnivorous seafaring iguana chewing winsomely on my innards, its black tuberculate scales glittering turquoise above the eddying brine. Its companions licked our bones clean, sated on our succulent flesh. We had hired a bush pilot to drop us at a remote shore far beyond the cloying scent of nocturnal cyclamen. We were like exhausted gamblers reclining on a bloodstained dune, our conveyor-belt romance continuously threatening to deliver. It would never be enough, and yet we were gripped by an ominous fever which routinely failed to break. It is a preparation for the afterlife. Purgatory? Death is too paltry for us to refuse. It would never be enough. I have no recourse to vulgar aesthetics. *We need you to throw the gun out of the window.* Everybody loves you. It would never be enough — a visceral unconscious — humility, pain, and pleasure — the central metaphor of my life is gyrational perfidy. It would never be enough.

PSYCHOPATHIC COUPLES OF MY DREAMS: All was dead silence; I was comfortably in the adoptive saddle. Violence is our only means of dealing with reality. There are no judgements or morals behind our crimes. It is an eruption of repression that manifests itself by causing the death of others. *What does a life of false testimony really matter?* Only idiots tell the truth, and only lovers die alone. Have you ever seen a deadly box jelly devouring a witless fish? My masters and mistresses would attest to the authenticity of my various transformations. In the midst of this idyll, we removed the vodka-drenched heart and lungs from Vladimir Nabokov's bloated corpse. We removed half of the rib-cage and steaks. Maggots already! We hauled the entrails to a cave and dumped the rest in a polluted rivulet. An idealogue in the form of a vast nematocyst rose to greet us. Inexplicably, it had contrived to navigate upstream having followed us all the way from the old ocean. Maldoror we had confined to his matchbox. This place here is mountainous, bare of trees and the climate is rough. People brought here die quickly and quietly in the dun-coloured steppes of grass. They are skewered. A sharpened stake or metallic pole is inserted into their rectums. Their intestines are pierced. Ideally the pole penetrates from anus to mouth. I've only ever seen it adequately illustrated in obscure Uruguayan cartoons commemorated on increasingly rare postage stamps. *This is where corporate warriors come to die; all the money in the world won't cure them or alleviate their profound infirmity,* she announced. *These people are all inflicted with the debilitating malady known as vapid conformity masquerading as prodigious hubris. They are weak and deserve to be ruthlessly exterminated. The Mayans, Olmecs and Aztecs knew a thing or two about human sacrifice.* I silently sipped my Ribena, not daring to utter a single solitary slovo. Beetle-browed, Maldoror raged inside his miniature cardboard cell — a phosphorescent beam emerged from between the cracks —

AN INTENSE SHIFT: You could say I live in the shadow of my glamorous mother. My performances failed to blow her away but my refinement and comfort kept her coming back for more. She said my fragile exterior, gauche mannerisms and innocent expression masked a deeper pathology that would prove to be my most enduring and endearing quality. I'd spent months at an exclusive finishing school secreted in the bewitching wilderness of the Gaspé Peninsula. I returned fluent in Québécois French and armed with an impressive array of talents. I was the best flower arranger and eider hunter in the whole of Nine Elms, which was, as we all know, famously bombed by extremists. Ignoring my protests, she confined me to a small attic room, sending young adolescent boys up to visit me during those seemingly interminable hours. They had each been diagnosed with various learning difficulties and behavioural issues. They took me for a most likely companion and contemporary, happily molesting me all summer long. They loved to pull the ribbons from my hair and yank on my Dutch braids. Dazzling windows of diamonds rise up all around us. We stroll along the boulevards, hand in hand, fingers interlaced. ♫ *Feel me now — feel the pain — take the blame* ♫ This is Paris. Oh Paris. Trying to impress you, I commit the cardinal error of joking about the death of a princess. I am rewarded for my indiscretions much later when you spoon-feed me ice cream on the terrace overlooking the Seine. Your husband throttles me and cuts open my left wrist simply to watch me bleed into a small porcelain teacup. He later apologises, saying *I got a bit carried away* and I reply, *it's okay, I don't mind.* If none of this is even real why do I have to feel this way? A ribbon of stars flutters across the midnight sky. Pizza pie. *Amore.*

LAZY TRASH NARRATIVE: Tucked gently into my warm Procrustean bed, I dream that I am a nuclear missile flying high above the Atlantic Ocean towards New York. I'm twisting and turning in the air and Manhattan is looming on the horizon all lit up and it looks so alluring until I see 432 Park Avenue and I'm heading straight for it and I close my eyes resigned to the inevitable and I plough right into it and the whole building explodes and I become the nuclear explosion and the whole of Manhattan gets totally flattened and the night sky is glowing orange and red and my spirit soars high above it all and the biggest mushroom cloud I've ever seen in my entire life forms in a tremendous billowing of smoke and flames on an unprecedented scale and as I'm floating around just a ghost a flying saucer decorated with the North Korean flag arrives and these tiny little aliens accuse me of being a tabloid simulator and suck me with an electric laser thing into a metal box and I'm trapped inside and they sling me over their shoulder and the next thing I know I'm in a museum somewhere in Pyongyang surrounded by all the descendants of Joe Dresnok. They brush my hair as I recline on a marble slab and smother me with smoochie-kiss-kissies. We eat kimchi bokkeumbap and I impress them with my skilful use of silver chopsticks. They present me with a charming tortoiseshell barette which I immediately clip into my hair. The best things in life are free. *Juche* versus *Sadae,* bizarre n'est-ce pas? Then Kim Jong-un comes in drinking from a crystal carafe of cognac but it's Vladimir Nabokov in disguise and he looks like a ripe wet watermelon but his fly is open and I say *hey granddaddy that's poshlost* and then I wake up.

THEY GENERALLY FAVOUR WARM SEAS MORE THAN 35KM FROM THE COAST WHERE THE WATER IS SALTIEST: Lifelong specialists and enthusiasts, jellyfish prefer warmth and salinity and usually travel in gelatinous swarms. Ever since I was a child I was fascinated by these creatures, but it wasn't until that fateful August afternoon the day before my fifteenth birthday that I discovered I was sexually attracted to them too. My bedroom wall was covered in photographs of jellyfish rather than boys (or girls) but my parents never suspected a thing. Experiencing a dearth of information — even online — and in the absence of access to psychotherapeutic support, I gradually came to terms with the indisputable fact that I was a *medusozoaphile* — not to be confused with *methuselaphiles* or even *mezuzahphiles* (we were once described as cnidariaphrodites but that term is now unsurprisingly regarded as dated and offensive). I began to explore my fantasies in quiet seclusion, deriving an erotic charge from perusing video images of these wondrous sea jellies on YouTube. Later I visited various aquaria all around the world, becoming steadily more aroused until I could bear it no longer and began to stealthily masturbate in front of the glass. In Tokyo, neatly and demurely disguised as an unassuming Japanese schoolgirl, I climaxed covertly whilst admiring a smack of spotted jellies glide through the irradiated water, their pulsating bioluminescent bells and trailing tentacles moving me to heights of juvenile ecstasy. Reality and fantasy are sometimes separated by only the thinnest of membranes, I reflected pensively. I longed to drown myself in the old ocean, with innumerable jellyfish surrounding me, their tentacles caressing my flesh, their stinging cells playfully agonising my nipples and excruciating my clitoris.

I hereby declare that all of the information I have provided is categorically complete and correct to the best of my knowledge and that I have absolutely no need of a neoprene suit.
— Audrey Szasz, 21st June 2021, Trois-Rivières, QC, Canada

Contributor Biographies

Mark Amerika is the author of many literary books including *The Kafka Chronicles* (University of Alabama Press / FC2, 1993), *Sexual Blood* (University of Alabama Press / FC2, 1995), *29 Inches* (Chiasmus Press, 2007) and *Locus Solus* (Counterpath Press, 2014). His experiments in "theoretical critifiction" include META/DATA: A Digital Poetics (MIT Press, 2007), remixthebook (University of Minnesota Press, 2011) and remixthecontext (Routledge, 2018). His forthcoming book, *My Life as An Artificial Creative Intelligence*, will be published by Stanford University Press in 2022.

Louis Armand is the author of the novels *The Garden* (2020), *Vampyr* (2020) & *The Combinations* (2016). In addition, he has published collections of poetry, including *East Broadway Rundown* (2015) & *Monument* (with John Kinsella, 2020), & the collage-hybrid *Glitchhead* (2021). He lives in Prague. www.louis-armand.com

Ben Arzate lives in Des Moines, IA. He is the author of the novels *The Story of the Y* and *Elaine*, the short story collection *The Complete Idiot's Guide to Saying Goodbye*, and the poetry collections *dr. sodom and mrs. gomorrah* and *the sky is black and blue like a battered child*. His first book of plays is forthcoming. He is a regular contributor to Cultured Vultures and Babou 691. Find him online at dripdropdripdrop-dripdrop.blogspot.com

duncan b. barlow is the author five books including *A Dog Between Us* and *The City, Awake*. He is the Publisher at Astrophil Press and the Managing Editor at *South Dakota Review*. For more information regarding writing and music, go to: www.duncanbbarlow.com

Tosh Berman is a writer and poet, as well as the publisher of TamTam Books. He wrote *TOSH: Growing Up in Wallace Berman's World*, *Sparks-Tastic*, and a book of poems *The Plum in Mr. Blum's Pudding*. He is also the co-host of BOOK MUSIK podcast. You can follow Tosh's writings at https://tosh.substack.com

RJ Dent is a poet, novelist, translator, essayist, and short story writer. As a renowned translator of European literature, R J Dent has published modern English translations of *The Flowers of Evil* (Baudelaire), *The Songs of Maldoror* (Lautréamont), *Poems & Fragments* (Alcaeus); *The Dead Man* (Bataille), as well as significant works by Guillaume Apollinaire, Louis Aragon, Antonin Artaud, Andre Breton, Paul Celan, Paul Éluard, Maurice Heine, Maurice Rollinat, the Marquis De Sade and Tarjei Vesaas. As a poet and novelist, R J Dent is the author of a poetry collection, *Moonstone Silhouettes*, a novel, *Myth*, and a short story collection, *Gothiques and Fantastiques*. Authors that R J Dent admires include Jeremy Reed, Pascale Petit, Stephen Barber and Philippe Djian. R J Dent's official website is www.rjdent.com

Douglas Doornbos writes fiction and draws a mean maze. He lives in Minnesota.

Seb Doubinsky is a bilingual writer born in Paris in 1963. His novels, all set in a dystopian universe revolving around competing cities-states, have been published in the UK and in the USA. He currently lives with his family in Aarhus, Denmark, where he teaches at the University.

Steve Finbow's works include *Grave Desire: A Cultural History of Necrophilia* (Zero Books, 2014), *Notes from the Sick Room* (Repeater Books, 2017), *Death Mort Tod: A European Book of the Dead* (Infinity Land Press, 2018) and *The Mindshaft* (Amphetamine Sulphate, 2020). He is currently ekphratic and living in Kingston upon Thames.

Chris Kelso is a British Fantasy Award-nominated genre writer, illustrator, and anthologist. His work has been published in *3AM magazine, Black Static, Locus, Daily Science Fiction, Antipodean-SF, SF Signal, Dark Discoveries, The Scottish Poetry Library, Invert/Extant, The Lovecraft e-zine, Sensitive Skin, Evergreen Review, Verbicide*, and many others. He has been translated into French and is the two-time winner of the Ginger Nuts of Horror Novel of the Year (in 2016 for *Unger House Radicals* and 2017 for *Shrapnel Apartments*). *The Black Dog Eats the City* made Weird Fiction Reviews Best of 2014 list. *Shrapnel Apartments* was endorsed by Dennis Cooper on his blog, "4 Books I read and Loved."

Faisal Khan is a writer and illustrator based in the suburbs of

Atlanta.

Dylan Krieger is writing the apocalypse in real time in south Louisiana. She earned her BA in English and philosophy from the University of Notre Dame and her MFA in creative writing from Louisiana State University. Her first book, *Giving Godhead* (Delete, 2017), was dubbed "the best collection of poetry to appear in English in 2017" by the New York Times Book Review. She is also the author of *Dreamland Trash* (Saint Julian, 2018), *No Ledge Left to Love* (Ping Pong, 2018), *The Mother Wart* (Vegetarian Alcoholic, 2019), *Metamortuary* (Nine Mile, 2020), *Soft-Focus Slaughterhouse* (11:11, 2021), and a vinyl EP called *Turn into the Water* (Fine Print, 2020). Find her at dylankrieger.com or dylankriegerpoetry.bigcartel. com

Callum Leckie is a 35-year-old working class Mancunian (estate boy) & bibliophile who draws pictures. callumleckie2017. tumblr.com

Chris Lloyd is a Berlin-based concert pianist, curator, author, and co-founder of the international interdisciplinary movement, Crossmodalism. Lloyd is passionate about radical disruption and change within the traditional classical music industry. Aside from performance, he is currently writing his first book (published by Repeater Books Ltd., U.K.) exploring the existing flaws with the traditional system, and writes regularly for Interlude.HK (Hong Kong), Classeek Showroom (Switzerland) and Limelight Magazine (Australia). In 2018 he founded the 1781 Collective, whose mission is to explore new methods of classical music performance driven by the motto: "Why play along with their system, when we can just create our own?" More information at www.chrislloydpianist. com and www.1781collective.com

Alexis Lykiard is a Greek-born poet and novelist who has translated what is to date the first and only fully-annotated edition in English of Lautréamont-Ducasse's *Complete Works*. The current reprint is available from publishers Exact Change, USA. Details of this and Lykiard's many other books can be found on www.alexislykiard.com

Jennifer MacBain-Stephens graduated from the Tisch School of the Arts at NYU and now lives in Iowa. She is the author of four full length poetry collections and fifteen chapbooks.

She enjoys writing about the natural landscape and finds inspiration in surrealism and horror movies. Recent work can be read in *Grist, Dream Pop, The Westchester Review,* and *Angel Rust*. She also hosts a monthly reading series called *Today You are Perfect*. Find her at JenniferMacBainStephens.com

Chris Nelms lives in Beaufort, South Carolina and writes when he can.

Golnoosh Nour is the author of *The Ministry of Guidance and Other Stories* – recently nominated for the Polari Prize. Her first poetry book was published in 2017. Her poetry collection *Rocksong* will be published in October 2021 by Verve Poetry Press. Golnoosh's work has also been published in Granta, selffuck, Columbia Journal, and Poetry Anthology amongst others. Golnoosh has performed her work across the UK and internationally. She teaches Creative Writing at the University of Reading. She's the co-editor of Magma 80 and the anthology *Queer Life, Queer Love* forthcoming with Muswell Press.

Jeremy Reed is one of the most exciting, controversial and original of British poets, and his recent poetry collections include *Piccadilly Bongo, Sooner or Later Frank, Voodoo Excess, Candy4Cannibals, Psychedelic Meadow, I Never Said I Was Nice* and *Dungeness Blues*. His non-fiction books in recent years number *The Dilly: A Secret History of Piccadilly Rent Boys, Lou Reed Waiting For The Man, Altered Balance* and his London memoir, *Bandit Poet*. Famous for his electrifying poetry performances with the musician Itchy Ear as Jeremy Reed and the Ginger Light, their new CD, *Stalker,* is available from Moloko. Reed's novel from the 90s *Isidore* is the only fictional recreation of Lautreamont in English. He was called by the Independent "British poetry's glam, spangly, shape-shifting answer to David Bowie."

John Reed is the author of three novels, three works of illustrated non-fiction, one book of poetry, and one work by William Shakespeare. He has an MFA in Creative Writing from Columbia University, has been published in Art in America, the Paris Review, the Times Literary Supplement, the Wall Street Journal, Vice, the New York Times, and Harpers, and has been anthologized in Best American Essays. More at @ easyreeder & easyreeder.com

James Reich is the author of five novels, most recently *The*

Song My Enemies Sing (Anti-Oedipus Press). He serves as chair of Creative Writing and Literature at New Mexico School for the Arts, in Santa Fe, NM and is the founder and editor at Stalking Horse Press. His next full-length work, *Ego & Extinction: Science Fiction and Ecopsychology* is scheduled for publication in 2022. Learn more at: www.jamesreichbooks.com

David Leo Rice is the author of the novels *A Room in Dodge City, A Room in Dodge City: Vol. 2,* and *Angel House*, as well as the just-published story collection *Drifter*. His next novel, *The New House*, is coming in 2022. He's online at: www.raviddice.com

Jordan A. Rothacker is a writer who lives in Athens, Georgia where he received a MA in Religion and a PhD in Comparative Literature from the University of Georgia. He also received a BA in Philosophy from Manhattanville College in Purchase, New York, the state in which he was born. His essays, reviews, interviews, poetry, and fiction have been featured in such publications as *The Exquisite Corpse, Guernica, Bomb Magazine, Entropy, Vol. 1 Brooklyn, Brooklyn Rail, Rain Taxi, Dead Flowers, Literary Hub*, and *The Believer*. Rothacker is the author of the novels: *The Pit, and No Other Stories* (Black Hill Press, 2015); *And Wind Will Wash Away* (Deeds, 2016); and *My Shadow Book by Maawaam* (Spaceboy Books, 2017); and the short story collection, *Gristle: weird tales* (Stalking Horse Press, 2019). For publishing news visit jordanrothacker.com

Audrey (aka Zutka) Szasz is a London-based writer, performer and sound designer with roots in Central Europe. Her experimental narratives combine vivid prose with exotic imagery and macabre satire. She has been described alternately as "the postmodern heir to the disarranged novels of Anna Kavan and more closely, Ann Quin," and "a deviant genius of surreal and perverse image-play." Audrey's debut in print, *Plan for the Abduction of J.G. Ballard* (a collaboration with author and poet Jeremy Reed) was published in 2019 via Infinity Land Press. In 2020, Amphetamine Sulphate issued her first solo novella, *Invisibility: A Manifesto*. Her debut full-length novel, *Tears of a Komsomol Girl*, was released in December 2020 by Infinity Land Press. In June 2021 Audrey's hour-long sound and spoken-word piece *Deposition: Agent Erdély* was published on the acclaimed Nearest Truth podcast, whilst her latest novella, *A-Z of Robomasochism*, is included in the Amphetamine Sulphate science fiction anthology *Human Rights*, set to be released in 2021.

Permissions

Tosh Berman quotes from:
-- Alexis Lykiard translation of Maldoror; quoted on pages 17-19; permission from Exact Change

RJ Dent quotes from:
-- Guy Wernham translation of Maldoror; quoted on page 22; permission from New Directions

-- Alexis Lykiard translation of Maldoror; quoted on pages 23; permission from Exact Change

-- Paul Knight translation of Maldoror; quoted on page 23; permission from Penguin Random House UK

Steve Finbow quotes from:
-- Alexis Lykiard translation of Maldoror; quoted on pages 32-33; permission from Exact Change

Faisal Khan quotes from:
-- William T. Vollmann interviewed by Madison Smartt Bell in Paris Review (issue 156, Fall 2000); quoted on page 37; permission from Paris Review

-- EM Cioran, The New Gods; quoted twice on pages 37-38; permission from University of Chicago Press

-- Franz Kafka in Diaries of Kafka 1910-1923; quoted on pages 38 and 42; permission from New Directions

-- Ibn Abbad, from Thomas Merton's Raids on the Unspeakable; quoted on page 40; permission from New Directions

-- Alexis Lykiard translation of Maldoror; quoted on pages 40; permission from Exact Change

-- JM Le Clezio, "Freedom to Dream," World Literature Today (vol. 71, no. 4, Autumn, 1997, pp 671-674; quoted on page 40; permission from World Literature Today

-- Aimee Cesaire, "Discourses on Colonialism;" quoted on page 41; permission from Monthly Review Press (2001)

-- Alejandra Piznarik, Extracting the Stone of Madness; quoted on page 41; permission from New Directions

Jennifer MacBain-Stephen quotes from:
-- Alexis Lykiard translation of Maldoror; quoted on page 57; permission from Exact Change

Jeremy Reed quotes from:
-- Alexis Lykiard translation of Maldoror; quoted on pages 69-75; permission from Exact Change

-- David Sylvester, The Brutality of Fact: Interviews with Francis Bacon © 1975, 1980, 1987, 1992 and 2016; quoted on pages 71; Reprinted by kind permission of Thames & Hudson Ltd., London.

Jordan A. Rothacker quotes from:
-- Roberto Calasso, Literature and the Gods; quoted on pages 1-2; permission from Penguin Random House.